Bastard

Royal Bastards MC Texas

WALL STREET JOURNAL & USA TODAY BESTSELLING AUTHOR

SAPPHIRE KNIGHT

Sapphire Knight

Bastard

Copyright © 2020 Bastard by Sapphire Knight

Editing by Mitzi Carroll

Formatting by Brenda Wright – Formatting Done Wright

This book is a work of fiction. The names, characters, places, and incidents are products of the writer's imagination or have been used fictitiously and are not to be construed as real. Any resemblance to persons, living or dead, actual events, locales or organizations is entirely coincidental.

All rights reserved. With the exception of quotes used in reviews, this book may not be reproduced or used in whole or in part by any means existing without written permission from the author.

The author acknowledges the trademarked status and trademark owners of various products referenced in this work of fiction, which have been used without permission. The publication/use of these trademarks is not authorized, associated with, or sponsored by the trademark owners.

WARNING

This novel includes graphic language and adult situations. It may be offensive to some readers and includes situations that may be hotspots for certain individuals. This book is intended for ages 18 and older due to some steamy spots. This work is fictional. The story is meant to entertain the reader and may not always be completely accurate. Any reproduction of these works without Author Sapphire Knight's written consent is pirating and will be punished to the fullest extent of the law.

- This book is fiction.
- The guys are over-the-top alphas.
- My men and women are nuts.
- This is not real.
- Don't steal my shit.
- Read for enjoyment.
- This is not your momma's cookbook.
- Easily offended people should not read this.
- Don't be a dick.
- Romance shaming is slut-shaming; don't be that asshole.

Dedication

Bastard is for everyone who fell in love with my MCs back in the day when I decided to publish them publicly. This book feels like old-school Sapphire to me, and I hope you all appreciate it. I loved this story, as it came out of nowhere, and those are always my favorites.

To new readers who are discovering me for the first time, I hope you fall down the rabbit hole and love every minute of it.

And finally, to my mother, who's six months clean and sober. I feel like I'm finally getting a chance to have a relationship with you for the first time in my adult life. I'm not usually the praying type, but I've been praying that you stick with it. I know it can't be easy when it's been a part of your life for so very long. But I like the person you are when you're like this.

Royal Bastard MC Code

PROTECT: *The club and your brothers come before anything else and must be protected at all costs. Club is family.*

RESPECT: *Earn it & Give it. Respect club law. Respect the patch. Respect your brothers. Disrespect a member, and there will be hell to pay.*

HONOR: *Being patched in is an honor, not a right. Your colors are sacred, not to be left alone, and never let them touch the ground.*

OL' LADIES: *Never disrespect a member's or brother's Ol' Lady.*

CHURCH: *It is mandatory.*

LOYALTY: *Takes precedence overall, including well-being.*

HONESTY: *Never lie, cheat, or steal from another member or the club.*

TERRITORY: *You are to respect your brother's property and follow their Chapter's club rules.*

TRUST: *Years to earn it...seconds to lose it.*

NEVER RIDE OFF: *Brothers do not abandon their family.*

Bastard is part of the Royal Bastard World. *Bastard* is not affiliated with any other books or Authors aside from being included in this world. You do not need to read any other books to read *Bastard*. I have not read all the other books in this world and am not responsible for sensitive subjects they may write about in their own stories.

RBMC TEXAS MEMBERS

Ripper – President

Blow – Vice President

Whiskey – Treasurer

Powerhouse – Sgt. At Arms

Angel - Enforcer

Plague – Member

Baker - Member

Wrench – Member

Ammo – Prospect sponsored by Powerhouse

Mouse – Prospect sponsored by Blow

Manic – Prospect sponsored by Plague

Lunatic – Prospect Sponsored by Angel

Special mention of:

Gamble – President

Character by Elizabeth Knox

Dog- deceased

Character by Elizabeth Knox

Rancid - President

Character by Crimson Syn

Common Terms

MC - Motorcycle Club

Ol' Lady – Female significant other

Chapel - Where Church is held

Clubhouse/ Compound – MC home base

Church - MC "meeting"

Bet – Yes, yep, yeah, okay, fuck yeah, hell yeah, that's what's up, …etc.

(You get the picture)

Sapphire Knight

Chapter 1

> Make peace with your broken pieces.
> -R.H. Sin

Another day, another dollar. It's what I tell myself every single day, especially when it comes to the dancers and the shit that goes down most of the time at the notorious strip club. I'm in the back room flirting with the girls as I always do when I notice a nice ass—currently clenched. She must be new, so I welcome her as I have all the previous girls. "Hey, doll, this your first night?"

She turns toward my voice, her eyes full of nervousness. "Yeah, I've danced before, …but not to a crowd like this."

I crack a grin and send her a wink, "No worries. I have just the thing to calm your nerves." Relief shines back, and her shoulders lose a bit of their tenseness. "Ladies, let's show the new chick how we like to warm up," I say to the room behind me, and a few giggles follow my request. They eagerly make their way over, as new girl watches, curiosity getting the best of her. I've been doing this for years since the owner, and I came to a mutual agreement. You pay up, and the Royal Bastards MC has your back. In his case, we protect his club and the girls when they need us to.

Flicking my button free, I tug my zipper down and pull my fat cock out. I flash the ladies a bright smile as I dig the glass vial free from my pocket. The white powder inside is enough to entice these dancers to do whatever the fuck I'd like. In this case, it has them on their knees before me. Wearing the patch of prez offers me those pleasures as well, but I don't throw my weight around from the club unless it's necessary. "All right, get in line, and no pushing," I mutter, carefully twisting the lid off. My cock's heavy enough it damn near juts out toward the floor from my hips. The motherfucker already knows we're headed to hell, so he's pointing the way.

Tapping the first generous line on my cock, the eager whore falls to her knees and snorts quickly, like the feaning freeloader she is. She follows it up with a slow lick across my shaft then gets up to allow the next woman to have her turn. This goes on three more times before it's finally the new chick's turn. It's her first time, so if she wants this little habit to continue, she'll have to finish sucking me off. It's enrapturing watching several women before me, all working on my pleasure. It's a heady feeling.

"On your knees, dancer." I gesture down and tip a generous amount of powder on the tip of my cock. She snorts a little into both nostrils and timidly sticks her tongue out toward my dick. A chuckle erupts from my chest and I shake my head. "Nuh-uh, you suck, and don't stop until I tell you to." She goes to work, and as I come, I give her the customary, "Welcome to BJ's Dollhouse. I'm Ripper, the Royal Bastards Prez, and I've got plenty more *soda*; you hit me up to buy."

Getting my cock sucked is a small price to pay for the MC's protection. Being Prez means I get worshipped more than the others, even the brothers that women would refer to as better looking, like Blow or Plague. I know I'm not hard on the eyes—been told that shit my entire life. I'm also not a fuckin' idiot and am well aware a few of my brothers beat me in that department. As long as I can still easily kick their asses, well, I ain't worried in the slightest. Pussy is easy, and it comes to me naturally. It's one of the things I love most about women. That new female down at the club wasn't so bad either. She's been on my mind ever since she swirled her tongue around the head of my cock a few nights back. I wouldn't mind having me some more of that, maybe dip between those thick thighs if she kindly offers.

"Powerhouse!" I yell for my sergeant at arms (SAA).

"Prez?" He comes barreling into the storeroom as I'm taking inventory. The product is getting low; it's almost time for my VP to hit up our contact and bring in some more coke. Our ganja runner should be stopping in this week as well. The club owns a storage facility to help bring in a side income. It also fronts for the more illegal businesses we take part in.

"Head down to BJ's and pick up that new bitch. She gave some good head, and I'd like a reminder."

"Maddy?" he asks kindly. For being a big oaf, he's sweet on the dancers. Kind of like a puppy dog around them or some shit. Anywhere else and he's a force to be reckoned with. I don't mind it that he's a softy, as long as our enemies don't take notice. Lucky for us, we're not buried in club wars but tend to tolerate the MCs around here, and they do the same with us.

I shrug. "Fuck if I know, brother. Never caught her name, never cared. She was new and nervous, easy on the eyes. Those types always go to their knees quickly."

"Yeah, her name's Madison, but the girls been callin' her Maddy."

"Got it," I mutter, shifting around a few kilos. Not that I fucking care about her name, and it'd do him well to forget it as well. He's already got a thing for one of the dancers to the point I think it's an obsession.

"Anyone else?"

"You can see if a few of 'em want to come back to the club and make some extra cash. I'm sure you fuckers wouldn't mind some private dances."

He grins. "I'll see who's available and be back."

I wave him off, stuck in my head with the numbers.

"Ride safe."

We have a club brick in a lockbox in here that we use strictly for new clients to test and for when we party. Partiers have the option of buying small amounts, and it's accessible if the brothers need to replenish their stash. We aren't a club full of tweakers, by any means. It's one of our more lucrative businesses, and the brothers have been made well aware it's not an everyday thing. Blow's the one brother with a pass to do it whenever the fuck he wants, as he's my VP. If it gets out of hand, though, I'll put a stop to that shit quickly. Whiskey's the only one with a key to the box, so it allows me the chance to closely monitor the brothers' refills and sales through our notes.

I quickly scribble down on his sheet that I took two eight balls' worth. I transfer his latest notes onto my inventory paper and relock the box. I'll return the key to him shortly now that I have everything I need. I'm not only a hardened biker but also a businessman, and I don't fuck around when it comes to our product.

"Prez?" Whiskey pokes his head in the door.

"I'm here," I rumble, making my way to him. I hand over the key.

"That was fast."

I fold the sheet up and stick it in my wallet. It's numbers and letters, an easy code I came up with in case I ever get searched. It's happened in the past, so I know it'll most likely happen again. The cops love to pull us over and pat us down whenever given a chance. "We're low on everything, so it was easy. I've got deliveries already in the works. I've gotta get Blow to reach out to Jersey too. It's time to take in more kilos."

"You want me to talk to him?"

I shake my head. "Nah, he'll be around later. I hit up Powerhouse to collect some girls; you know Blow can't stay away when there's pussy and cocaine nearby."

He chuckles, running a hand over his beard peppered with gray. He's in his early fifties, and seeing him age more these last few years has me thinking on the long-term side of things. We need to keep on the path we are now. If we stick to it, we won't have to worry about this shit when I'm older. The brothers can be comfortable without risking their necks. The last thing I wanna do is be locked up for a chunk of my life, but I'll peddle the drugs if it means we'll be all right down the road.

"He better watch he doesn't knock one of them up. Those bitches flock to his dick like it's chocolate or some shit."

I cough out a laugh. I wasn't expecting that tidbit to come from him. "Fuck, man, I didn't need that image in my mind."

He chuckles, offering a shrug. He's not sorry in the least. Fucker. "Spoke to your old man."

"Oh, yeah? That bastard calls you but not his son."

"He's riding along the coast, sucking up that salt air."

"Lucky bastard. I bet my mom's happier than shit having him all to herself. They'll be back home soon enough. My pops can't be gone from the garage for too long, or he loses his shit."

He grunts, agreeing. "We could always set up our own ride; it's been a while."

"Maybe down the road, but we have too many consistent sales going on right now. I want our *fedia* to flourish, and our pockets to fill before we fuck off and roll out for weeks on end. Once we start, we may not return for who knows how long."

"That's the beauty of it—the freedom."

"Couldn't agree more. We'll plan something soon, even if it's only a short ride down to the gulf for some cold beer and salty air."

He nods, appearing less stressed already. Blow may be my VP, but Whiskey takes on a brunt of the club responsibilities as well. He's the club treasurer but also acts as the secretary as well. He's got his hands dipped into everything, as do I. Blow's my best friend, but he's got less obligation, and he likes it that way. He gets the respect of rank, but the freedom to fuck off when he wants, the lucky bastard.

A text comes through, and I toss a pleased grin at Whiskey. "Powerhouse has a truckload of bitches. It looks like we'll have some entertainment soon enough."

"Mm, guess I better eat a sandwich. You young assholes like to binge drink without eating. I can't handle that shit anymore."

I chuckle and salute him as he heads for the small kitchen. We binge drink without eating cause it gets you fucked up faster. I don't on every occasion; it depends on Powerhouse and if he's partying or not. He keeps an eye on things most times, but some nights I have him cut loose, and I sip slowly, making sure shit doesn't head south. I won't put our club in jeopardy just to party, even if we are a pretty wild bunch. With everyone doing their own thing, I head for my shower. I want my cock sucked tonight, and bitches love a good smelling man.

Chapter 2

*If we were meant to stay in one place,
we'd have roots instead of feet.
- Unknown*

Alice

"Have you found her yet?" my father demands, worry and anger coating his voice. He's the calm, rational one of our family, but lately, that role has fallen to me.

"I'm sorry, but I haven't. This place is crawling with people. It's almost impossible to get any leads unless you're constantly paying people. Majority of the time, the so-called leads turn out to be lies from people taking advantage of the situation. Sadly, people will lie so easily when it comes to a missing person."

"I think it's time you leave Nevada and head for Texas."

"Texas? You believe she's gotten that far?" My sister isn't exactly resourceful, but somehow, she's been finding ways to stay under the radar. Could she have met someone who's helping her? I suppose anything's possible at this point. I don't bring that suggestion up to my father. I can't stand to worry him any more than he already is.

"It's Madison. She always figures out a way to run. It's nearly election season, and I need her home, cleaned up and ready to play the dutiful daughter. If the press were made aware of these excursions she goes on, I'd be finished. Our family name would be tarnished. She thinks she hates life in politics; she'd hate it, even more, being poor. I was too easy on her as a little girl. I allowed your mother to give her whatever she wanted, and now I'm being punished for it. You were the good girl, Alice, always swimming and doing well with your studies. This is my punishment for having a wonderful family, I suppose."

"I know, Dad, but it's Madison. She's different. She doesn't think like we do. And stop taking this out on yourself; you've done nothing but try to protect us. She may've been spoiled, but you made sure we've always felt safe."

"Do not make excuses for her! She's tearing this family apart, all in the name of a spoiled tantrum."

"I'm not—"

"Look, honey, it's not only Madison that concerns me; it's you. I need you back here too. I don't like having both of my daughters so far away. You've always been a big help with my campaign, and I don't enjoy sending you on a wild goose chase. It's dangerous." My poor father...his emotions are all over the place, and he must be far more stressed out than I'd suspected. I have to find my sister.

"I have the security detail with me. I'm fine. So far, no one has recognized me, so everything is okay. I'm okay. I'll find Madison and come home as soon as possible. The campaign won't suffer."

"That's my girl. I know I can count on you. I've checked your account and added more money. Tell Richardson to head to central Texas next. I'll have Jenkins send over the latest leads on your sister's whereabouts. And, by all means, remain undetected."

"Okay, I will, Dad." Like he needs to remind me. I've lived in jeans, plain shirts, ball caps, and ponytails this entire trip. I feel like a teenager all over again—always in disguise so we could travel without being harassed. My father's been an influential man for as long as I can remember, and that comes with its ups and downs. We already had to be careful when traveling and such, being as wealthy as we are. Throw in the fact that my father is running for various offices, and the danger level shoots up several notches.

"Love you, sweetheart. We'll talk soon."

"Love you too. Bye," I reply and meet Richardson's knowing gaze. He's been on this hunt with me before, but so far, this has been the longest search. My younger sister likes to pull a disappearing act at least once a year, so this is nothing new to our family. Sometimes I think she was born to the wrong parents; she would've had a better chance at happiness with a regular life. Our mother and father have always had one goal in sight, and that's to rise to the top. Madison has been more of a hindrance to that goal than anything else, and it makes me empathetic toward her. I can't blame her for it. I have days when I wish my life were different, as well. Unlike her, I haven't acted on it before, but in a way, I think she's brave to search for what she wants.

"I'm sure you caught part of that," I mutter to Richardson when the call ends.

He nods. "Did I hear Senator Compton correctly when he said central Texas?"

"Yes, we're headed south. Too bad we're in these circumstances; it'd be the perfect opportunity to make our presence known in Dallas. Dad could use the positive exposure in the state, but that won't happen with Madison missing. She's the top priority."

"Why do you continue to search for her? This is like the fourth time since I've been working for your father. It's not your responsibility."

"She's my sister," I respond adamantly. "That's reason enough, and she is partly my responsibility. It's what sisters do."

"You're good to your family. I just hate to see them take advantage of that."

I shrug. "I'm used to it."

"I know, Alice. That makes it so much worse. You're a good woman; you don't deserve the headache. You should be next to your father right now. Someday you'll be the one campaigning in his place. You have so many ideas on how to help our state, and no one gives you the respect you deserve. You're an asset, not a private bounty hunter."

"Someday, Richardson, maybe. Until then, I have my sister to worry about. Last time, she was shacked up with that Russian drug dealer. There's no telling where she is now. She could be dead right now...that's what scares me the most. I just need to find her, see that she's all right, then I can worry about myself."

"Yes, ma'am; we'll find her." He offers me a reassuring smile. His chestnut hair is all over the place from dragging his hands through it while he drives us around.

"Thanks, Richardson," I murmur, and he speaks into his wrist, relaying the new direction to the set of guys in the car behind us. While he's quietly conversing with them, Jenkins sends me a text with the name and zip code of the new town. I change the car's GPS for Richardson and hit 'go' on the screen. It immediately sprouts off the next turn in a British accent and tells us our arrival will be at five a.m. My father had his car guy program it like that, especially for me because her slang makes me laugh.

Richardson tells his men the new location, and I close my eyes. Leaning my seat back, I allow my mind to wander. I need rest. Too much stress and worrying always wear me out. He turns on a classical piece I enjoy and keeps the volume low enough not to disturb me. The comfort from the

Cadillac's leather seats, the dark windows, and the sweet melody from the piano lull me to sleep.

"We're here, Alice." I'm shaken awake. That was a long, boring ride, and I must've dozed off again.

"Here?" I mumble, half awake. "I thought you said six more hours."

I'm met with Richardson's amused grin. "Yes, ma'am. We're in the middle of Texas. To be more precise, we're in the city of Pflugerville. We passed a cool looking water park, but you were sleeping pretty hard, so I didn't want to wake you yet."

"Thanks, errm, is this our hotel?" I drag my eyes around the lot, sleepily taking in my surroundings.

He nods. "Yes, and we're all checked in."

"Stopping last night was a good idea; I feel like I just had a power nap. You must be sick of driving, though, and sore from sitting."

He shrugs. "I'm at your disposal. It's my job to be here for you, so don't hesitate if you need me to pick up something for you."

I nod. I've heard it before from my father. These three guys he's dubbed as my security team have bent over backward to make sure I have whatever I need, and I appreciate them for it. "You guys take the evening to eat, sleep, and recoup. That was a long drive."

"I'm fine from the short nap last night." We stopped, so he and the other driver could get a bit of sleep. They push themselves too much, in my opinion.

"Richardson...I don't want to wear you out. You may be a highly trained bodyguard, but even the strongest guys need rest and substance."

"But—"

I cut him off. "Don't worry about me. I promise I'll stay in the hotel, and if I order anything, I'll have it sent to your room first. I know the drill."

"Not just in the hotel, in your room." He grows serious.

I may not be as sneaky as my sister, but my team has learned to watch my wording. By 'in the hotel,' I mean that I'll go anywhere on the property. They learned it the hard way, and so did I when they called my father worried for their jobs and my safety. "I was thinking of taking a swim."

His eyes bug. "Ma'am, then we definitely need to be present."

"I know how to swim...well, I might add."

"We know, Alice; we've seen the trophies at your father's estate. Even with your experience, you never know when someone may've picked up on our trail or who might recognize you."

"You think they'd drown me?" I ask, a bit outraged at the horror. I'm not naïve. I know not everyone cares for my father, but I've never wronged anyone. At least, not enough for them to attempt to viciously drown me.

"Amongst kidnapping, we have to take precaution. This is nothing new."

"I know, but this is the first I'm hearing of this! Who wants to drown me?"

"There've..."

"Tell me."

"There've been a few threats toward your family, all aimed at your father running for senator again."

"Toward me?"

He nods tightly, a fierce expression plastered across his normally calm features. "I was supposed to keep this information from you, but it may be the key to saving your life. Please don't tell Senator Compton, or you may have a new security detail flying out to take our place stat."

"I'll keep this to myself; you have my word." Dad used to have a female with me at all times, but that stopped when I got older and demanded my privacy. I'm an adult, and he has no reason not to trust me. I'm not Madison. He selected these three guys, in particular. They have my best interest in mind, and I won't jeopardize it, no matter how good a swim sounds to me right now.

I give in to the call of the water and ask, "If one of you doesn't mind, I'd like to take a swim at some point."

"Of course," he immediately agrees. "I will speak to the hotel manager and see if I can get us in at ten-thirty. The pool closes at ten, so you'll have it to yourself."

"Thank you." I offer a smile, though it wouldn't be so bad if other people were around. Especially children, I love seeing their excitement when it comes to swimming and splashing around. "I'll take my laptop inside with me and see what I can find out about this place while you all rest."

"Sounds like a plan. If you want food, please have one of us to order it for you. The extra precaution will make me feel better."

"Right." I offer a tight smile because, apparently, even ordering food on the telephone with a fake name is dangerous. Why didn't my father feel the need to bring this up if it's so serious? This pisses me off like no other, but I respect my father, so he must have his reasons.

My detail walks me to my room, checking the inside once more before leaving me alone with my laptop and suitcase. They didn't offer up a keycard or anything, and it has me feeling more like a prisoner than the senator's daughter. I call my sister's number like I do every day at this time, but Madison doesn't answer. She never answers, and as far as I know, she doesn't have a phone connected to the number, or else my dad would track her. I still call, just in case, and at the same time, so she can rely on me. She has access to her voicemail, so I hope she hears my messages and, at some point, calls me back.

With a disappointed sigh, I decide on a long, hot soak in the tub before I do some detective work. It should keep me busy enough, along with a call to my mom. The poor woman is kept out of the loop without my updates. It's cruel of my father, but he swears it's for my mother's own good. He doesn't want to worry her and stress her out when a lead turns to nothing. I get it; however, I don't agree with him, so I call her with details, and she pretends to be clueless around my father. She loves him enough to act like she's going along with his wishes, but she's always kept up to speed. Madison and I get our rebellious streak from her, and stubborn women like us always find a way to get what we want.

Chapter 3

> Hell is empty and all the
> devils are here.
> - William Shakespeare

Ripper

"Everything cherry at BJ's?" I ask as Powerhouse plants his ass next to me. I'm drinking a beer out back behind the club, chilling in the silence. I've got a small fire going in the pit before us—perfect on a chilly night like tonight. We've got some stumps and lawn chairs strewn about for the brothers, and whoever else may be around. Some nights we'll come out here to shoot the shit around a fire. It's relaxing, especially if you're hungover.

"Yeah, all good, Prez."

The owner pays us to help out with any issues he may have. Powerhouse throws his bulk around once a week to put a little fear into the customers messing with the strippers. He'd be there watching them dance regardless, so he may as well make some cash while doing it. Rarely do we all need to be there busting heads, but occasionally, we all show up to make our presence known. The owner doesn't mind if we invite the strippers back to the MC for a private performance, either. It gives the females a chance to make some extra *fedia,* and in return, they stay working for his wrinkly perverted ass longer.

"You were there a lot this week," I mention. All the brothers noticed—not just me. I don't want him to grow too attached to the strippers. He's fixated on watching them whenever he can. "You have a favorite or something?"

"There were a few new guys; some suits that I was keeping an eye on. They were too clean-cut to be in there. I wasn't sure if they were gonna fuck up one of the dancers."

"Ah. You find out who the fuck they are? Were they selling anything or peddling in flesh?"

He shakes his head. "They kept to themselves, didn't bother anyone. Maybe, since it's not far from the airport, they were looking for easy pussy."

I rub my face, not thinking too hard on it. "Should've had the girls grab their wallets. Could've gotten paid and had their names."

A devilish grin pulls at his lips. "I didn't feel like burying the bodies, or I would've."

A chuckle leaves me as I shake my head. He's a crazy fucker, and I don't doubt it for a minute that he's telling the truth. "Speaking of getting paid, that sale I was waiting on came through. Plague and Whiskey went out to meet our supplier and brought in some more powder. On the way home, they met with our big buyer and was able to get rid of a chunk they had on hand."

He whistles through his teeth, before commenting. "A kilo and a half, right? Same as last time? A twenty-one-k payday?"

"We cut him a deal and came home with eighteen profit."

"Nice."

"As always, Whiskey and Plague will take a higher cut since they risked their necks on pickup and drop off, but we'll still see some cheddar."

"That's what's up," he nods, cracking his knuckles and rolling his shoulders.

"We've got two weeks until another drop comes through, but I'll hit you up to see if you want in. Plague wants the cash, but he knows the rules—we offer the option to another brother first since he had last dibs. We'll discuss it in church next week. Make sure you hit up the strippers with baggies—a few of them been texting me about wanting to buy. I told them you'd come around when we got more in."

"I can do that, but I'll pass on the next exchange if someone else wants it. I've got a fight booked, so I have extra cash coming in."

"Sweet! Out at Hell Hole?"

He nods. The Hell Hole is an old biker bar out in bum fuck Egypt. It was built to surround an outside patio, but when the place started going to shit, they turned it into an outdoor fighting ring. It's reserved for MCs only and a decent place to make some money through personal bets. The owner's a lazy fuck and rarely opens anymore unless he has a fight in the works. It's a neutral ground where we all wear our colors and don't start shit with anybody unless we're willing to take it to the ring. The availability to bash someone's face in tends to keep the peace. Shit, I've been there when clubs have gone head to head and beat the shit out of each other one after the other. It makes for some good entertainment and contacts.

"You know who you're fighting?"

"Skull Cracker from Lost Saints."

My brows shoot up. "Thought you were cool with him."

"I am, but he threw out my name, and I responded."

"So, you'll be concentrating on training more?" That's another thing Powerhouse does all the time; the dude's way into fitness. We have a shelf full of shaker cups in his honor. The guy is always chugging something with protein in it.

He nods. "That a problem?"

"Not at all. I'm looking forward to watching you beat some ass."

He chuckles. "That you can count on."

"You hookup with anybody last week?" I ask, referencing the night he went and brought a truckload of strippers back for private entertainment.

He shrugs. "I got an eye on one of 'em. Not the one who was on your lap, though."

I shoot him a cocky smile. "Maddy's good at sucking my cock."

"I figured. She's been here every night since then," he points out, brow raised.

We hear moans coming from Blow's room. He's got his window open but blinds down. It sounds like he's going to town, too, and not holding back on her.

"Not only for me, man; she's been cozying up to Blow." I nod toward the open window and clear sounds of fucking. "I'm guessing they think I'm blind to her making heart eyes his way and shit. Not like he's being too careful about it; this shit happens a couple times a day. He may have a pretty face that bitches love, but my cock's still bigger."

He releases a hefty laugh and nods. "True that." We'd had a dick measuring contest one night when the shit-talking got out of hand. It's wasn't only a bunch of dudes and dicks, either. There were chicks present doing the measuring. Just another crazy night at the MC. Anyhow, it's been noted that I'm well-endowed—more so than any other motherfucker here. Hence my name, Ripper. It's not for removing heads; it's for tearing up pussy—one of my favorite things to do.

I shrug. "Wouldn't be surprised if she's making rounds. Bitches love an outlaw in their bed. Something about the danger of us keeps 'em coming back for more. I rarely catch their names anymore. As far as I'm concerned, they're around here to get my dick wet...nothing more."

"You're a bastard, brother."

I flash a grin and agree, "Through and through. No use in denying it. Being tame never got me anywhere, so fuck that boring shit."

"You're real. I've always respected that. It's one of the reasons why I wanted to be in a club with you leading."

"Appreciate that, man." I lean over so we can bump knuckles.

"I'm gonna head out." He stands. The fucker's massive, so I have to tilt my head to stare at his face.

My brow raises, curious as to where he's off to on a boring-ass Tuesday night. "Got plans, brother?"

"I'm going to stop by BJ's."

"Damn, someone's pussy got you hooked." I smirk. Can't help it. We like to give each other shit on occasion.

His lips tilt into a grin. "Not yet, but hopefully, one day."

"All right, man, ride safe."

"Thanks, brother," he grumbles and heads around the building.

More moans come from Blow's window, and I stand with a huff. I'm not about to sit around here and listen to my brother fucking. They sound like a bunch of dying cats and shit with the wailing getting out of hand. With that thought, I head to the bar. A short glass of whiskey will have me sleeping peacefully.

Powerhouse shows up in my office days later, Blow at his side. It's right around the time I usually start my inventory. The brothers know I'm always here to keep up with business shit on Sundays. "We have a problem," he confesses, not appearing happy to admit it. My mind shoots to our warehouses and storage facilities. Last I checked, they were empty, but they could've been raided, I suppose. We like to have them empty to keep nosey fucks our of our business, and it gives us the freedom to pretend like they're full. In return, we filter in drug money to make it appear like storage payments and legit cash flow.

"That so?" I nearly growl. I don't like motherfucking problems, especially when it's bad enough it takes two of them to tell me about it. "I swear to Christ, Plague better not've gotten popped last night. Is that it? Is he locked up? Or is it one of the storage buildings? We get raided?"

Whiskey shoots me a look, shaking his head. Obviously, he knows where Plague is. Glad someone's got his location locked down. His family's been having issues. His mom's been cancer-stricken, and it's made him a bit flighty. Not only that, but it's made him ballsier, and he wants to dig his hands into anything dangerous he gets wind of. A member on the rails is not a good thing to have when you run drugs, but he's our brother, and we've gotta have his back.

"No," Powerhouse confirms, rubbing his palm over his freshly shaved head. He's got some tribal shit tatted on it like a junior Mike Tyson. He caught shit for it from us until he decked Plague, and that shut us all up. Plague was knocked the fuck out. We weren't about to have that happen to us as well. "Blow, you want to tell Prez what happened?" he offers, and I'd chuckle at him tossing Blow to the top dog if I wasn't so on edge about their news.

"I was at BJ's. House called me to bring in some more product. He'd sold out." He nods to Powerhouse. He's always called him *House* as a nickname, never mind that Powerhouse is already his road name. I whistle lowly through my teeth, my eyes flashing to Powerhouse. He nods to confirm that he made bank today at the strip club.

"That's what's up," I mutter, holding my fist out. Powerhouse bumps my knuckles then we train our attention back to Blow.

"I was having a drink, chilling. I wanted to stick around since there were so many buyers. I felt like House may need me for some reason." He shrugs. "Anyway, I found out one of the dancers is a runaway or something."

"The fuck?"

Blow nods, releasing a pent-up breath, "You know me, I acted like I didn't know what the fuck they were talking about. I let the chick asking give me as much information as she wanted to offer up freely."

"Mm," I grunt.

"Imagine my fucking surprise when I'm still telling her I don't know jack shit, and she lays a photo of Madison on the table. I nearly choked on my motherfucking drink. Fuck, brother! The bitch is running, and she's been right under our noses."

"Madison?" I repeat, dumbstruck, and straighten up a bit more. "You mean the bitch we've had sucking cock...Maddy?

He grumbles, confirming. "It was some woman I hadn't seen before. She came snooping around, asking for her. Says she needs to be found and quietly. Guess her dad's a senator or some shit."

My brow wrinkles. "The fuck would an uppity rich bitch be strippin'? It doesn't make any sense. You sure she said it was her father?"

"Yep, trust me, Prez. I thought the same motherfucking thing when I heard it myself."

"Have you talked to Maddy about it?"

He shakes his head. "Nah, if it's true, I may scare her off."

"Might be a good thing, if she's who this chick is claiming her to be and all."

He silently bristles, not agreeing. I'm not a dumb fuck. I know he's carved out a soft spot for her.

"What aren't you telling me, Blow?" I press my VP. Obviously, he's not coughing up everything he knows. "Out with it. I don't give a shit if you're fucking her too." I decide to just speak plainly. I don't like my VP keeping thoughts to himself on this chick because we've both been tapping her ass.

"Maddy likes her powder."

"Ah." The pieces suddenly click together. I should've guessed if she was shacking up with my VP when she wasn't busy sucking my cock, it'd be for some snow. "She an addict? She's been smart enough not to ask me for any...just taking when I offer."

He shrugs, jaw flexing. "I'm not one to call someone out on their vices."

"Understandable. I'm just gauging the amount of liability this stripper brings to the club with her presence."

"I won't let her get us into any shit." He grows defensive. Fucker has definitely gone soft on the bitch.

I chuckle. The bastard that I am won't hesitate to call him on his bullshit. "She's already brought in shit! Think about what you just told me about who her pops is. He could be buddy-buddy with the fucking FBI, for all we know. The last thing we need is government presence in our fucking clubhouse, brother. The bitch could be working for daddy. Politicians love bringing down criminals. Looks good on their ass-kissing resumes."

"She's not like that," he states firmly, his cheeks red from irritation. I don't buy it for a minute. I sell drugs. I'm a skeptic on everyone who isn't a member of this club.

"How do you know? You'd trust her with your life, or with ours? You'd do time for the bitch?"

"If I didn't trust her, I wouldn't have her pussy in my bed, on repeat. She'd be a hit it and quit it—"

"Yet, you keep going back, meaning..."

He nods, confirming my earlier thought that he's soft on her.

"You feel something for her?" I ask outright, not pussyfooting around it.

"Maybe."

"All right, then. I'll stop getting my cock sucked by her."

"It's not like that."

I snort. "Give me a fucking break. You had hearts in your eyes from the moment you saw her."

"Fuck off."

"Just callin' it like I see it. Now, where is this person who was asking around?"

"It's her sister…a real fancy bitch. Gave me her card, told me to call if I saw Maddy, only she calls her Madison."

"Did you?"

"Fuck, no. If Maddy wanted to reach out, she would. Her relationship with her family is none of my business, nor do I want it to be."

"Well, make it your business. We can't have her fucking daddy showing up here next. A bullet in a senator will raise all types of flags, and I'm not trying to do any time without a good enough reason. You feel me?"

"Yeah, I get you. I'll see what I can find out, but so far, she's said next to nothin' about her personal life."

"*You're* her personal life now. If she's warming your bed, she'll start opening up. Bitches always do. This one'll be no different."

"Consider it done."

I nod. "And leave the card. I'll see what Plague can find out once he's slept off his latest tequila binge or whatever the hell he's into."

He tosses the small cardstock on my desk and, with a salute, makes his way out the club office. Powerhouse nods toward the door and follows Blow.

I jot down the name and digits before turning to a silent Whiskey. The fool didn't say a word the entire time my VP was in here defending his new bed interest. "You catch all that?"

He rolls his eyes. "I may be older than you, but I'm not fucking deaf."

With a chuckle, I hold the card to him. "Then give this to Plague and get what I need."

He nods. "I'll get back to you tomorrow on it."

"Appreciate it," I grumble and watch him pocket the card. He pecks at his phone, ordering us some lunch.

My gaze falls to the name I'd scribbled.

Alice Compton 287-747-8990 cell

Don't think I've ever met an Alice before. Even her name sounds like she belongs to a fucking senator or on a magazine cover. We don't need this shit, but my brother seems pretty fucking smitten with Maddy-the-stripper-slash-cock-sucking-wailer, and we take women seriously in our club. If he wants her, then none of us will stand in his way.

Not sure I can say the same for this Alice person. The last thing I want to do is bring her attention to us, but if I don't, they could turn this into a missing person, and that'll lead them to us regardless. Those bitchy dancers can't be trusted, and they all know Maddy has sucked mine and my VP's cocks while at the strip club. Hell, they've all given us a bit of lip service. It'll put us at the top of her family and the authorities' lists as suspects. It seems like some sort of shit is always coming at us, so I shouldn't be surprised. I wonder if any of the dancers have fed Alice information already. I should send a brother there as well to do a little recon.

"Powerhouse!" I holler, and he ducks back into my office. The fucker is built like a goddamn brick house, hence his road name. The females at the club love his ass, so he's the perfect person to go snooping around.

"Prez?"

"I need you to head over to BJ's."

"We need the VIP section? Gonna cut loose tonight?"

I shake my head. "Nah, this is just you, brother. You heard Blow talking about that nosey bitch asking around town about Maddy. I need you to find out if anyone else told her about Maddy coming to the club. Be my eyes and ears on this." Those strippers gossip like their life depends on it, and if someone offers up a buck, they'll spill whatever details they have. There's no loyalty when their lives revolve around a quick payday.

He nods. "I can do that, Prez, no problem."

"And be discreet. If they don't know anything, I don't want them to become curious as well. Don't offer up knowledge for them to give, ya know what I mean?"

"Got it." He nods again. "Anything else?"

I shake my head. "Appreciate it, man." I should mention that he needs to pull his head out of his ass where the dancers are concerned, but I hold back. I'll let him live in his fantasy world with them a bit longer, but if they cross us, it'll come to an end.

"No problem. Give me a few hours."

"Bet. Ride safe."

He's out the door before I can say another word. I steeple my hands, staring at the name *Alice* and wait…it's all I can do, for now.

Chapter 4

> Out beyond ideas of wrongdoing and
> rightdoing there is a field.
> I'll meet you there.
> - Rumi

Alice

"It's been a week, and nothing so far. I've left my card with a few businesses, and the team has been checking bars and clubs in the evenings regularly. I don't think this is the spot, Dad. What made you think of this city in the first place?"

"I didn't say anything before. I didn't want to get your hopes up in case it was nothing. Madison checked her voicemail. Jenkins gets a printout weekly of any numbers that connect to her voicemail, and the latest she used pinged on a cell tower in that city."

"Wow, that's huge! I had no idea she was checking her messages."

"It's what had me suggesting Nevada last time, but that lead was weeks old. There's no telling how long she's been gone from there. She could've checked her voicemail in Nevada as she was leaving—the same with this Texas city. We have no idea. You could be hopping from place to place chasing her, or else she could check it when she first gets to a city. We just don't know her pattern, unfortunately."

I sigh, staring up at the off-white ceiling. "I'm just happy to know she's alive." My voice cracks, emotion clouding me. "I was getting worried. She's been gone longer than any time before. I don't like this, Dad. I want to see her."

"By four weeks," my father replies, telling me what I already know, and I clench my eyes shut. She needs to come home. Madison can barely function living a privileged lifestyle, so why would I expect her to stay afloat and alive on the run?

I clear my throat, attempting to reason. "Can Jenkins get us the coordinates to the specific tower the call pinged on? At least we could try narrowing it down to a smaller area and search any convenience stores or mom and pop type places. Maybe she's found a job at one of those shops that'll pay her under the table. She has to be doing something; surely, she'd have blown through the few thousand she took when she initially left."

"Already done, honey. That's why Richardson has you checked into that specific hotel, and you've been searching around it. She was right by you and the team at some point. I have Jenkins monitoring her voicemail log daily this week. If she calls in, we'll know, and Jenkins will notify Richardson immediately."

"I've never brought it up, and I hate to now, but what if we don't find her this time?"

"Alice," he rumbles, his voice strong and steady as always. "She's done this time and again. You know as well as I do, you'll find her."

"I'm just growing more anxious by the day that when I do, she'll be in a morgue somewhere. She's not prepared for the regular world, Dad. Madison is naïve and always manages to find trouble somehow."

"It's okay to be scared for her, sweetheart. You're the stronger one; you remind me of myself. I worry for her as well, but we're doing everything we can. Stay the course, Alice."

"Not everything; we could bring in the news and ask for their help."

He scoffs. "Please, Alice, the media would have a field day with this. It's too close to my campaign. We can't have a scandal of any kind."

"I know. Forget I mentioned it. I've got to go, Dad. I'm going to get something to eat with Richardson and double-check a few places the team stopped in when we first got to town."

"Keep up the good work, honey. We'll have a party when you get home if you'd like. You've earned it."

"Thanks, Dad." I can't think of parties or celebrations right now when my sister could be in danger and not realize it. If I have threats against me, then I'm sure they go for her as well. I'm surrounded by three trained men to protect me. She has no one. "I'll call you soon. Love you."

"Thanks, honey. Love you too," he replies and hangs up.

I immediately jump up and head over to the TV. I knock on the wall, signaling next door to Richardson that I'm ready. It takes him less than a minute, and I hear the click from him inserting my keycard in the lock.

"Alice?" he greets.

"Hey, I'm done. Let's get some food, and I want to check out those bars you guys went to when we first got into town."

He nods. I know he heard my conversation. I have an audio and GPS earring I wear so he can always hear me, no matter where I am. I remove it to shower, but it's for my protection, so I keep it on at all other times. He casts his eyes over me quickly and turns to leave. I can't help but wonder what he thinks of the red dress I chose for the occasion. I wear jeans and plain shirts paired with ball caps most days to keep me plain on the road and under the media's nose. When we go out, like today, I dress the part. Rather than looking like the usual townie or tourist, we appear to be on a date, eating and going for a drink. I need to find Madison without raising too many flags. I don't want her to end up on page six or alert any bad people of her presence.

I grab my Chanel clutch that has my card, Madison's photo, a fake ID, and fifty dollars. I keep it simple, so if I ever get robbed, I don't seem like anyone important. I'd be worth at least a couple million dollars if anyone ever wanted to kidnap me and hold me for ransom. That goes for Madison as well. I quickly touch up my Mac matte rouge lipstick on the way out, tossing the tube in my clutch as well and meet Richardson in the hall.

"All clear," he reassures, and I flash a grateful smile. "What would you like to eat?"

My shoulders lift in a noncommittal shrug. "Surprise me with something along the way to this bar."

"It's a strip club, ma'am."

"I know. It just sounds more pleasant being called a club or bar. Besides, my father would lose it if he knew she usually ends up in strip clubs dancing. I was floored the first time we found her like that, and I'm sure he'd have a heart attack thinking of his baby girl in that position."

"Of course. You have my team's silence."

"Thank you. I know I can count on you guys. You three certainly make all this searching more bearable."

He grins and opens my door. I slide into the comfortable seat of the luxury sedan that's become a home away from home for me. I buckle up and fix my dress as he rounds the car and hops in behind the wheel. I watch the scenery as he drives in the direction of the airport. The strip club's not exactly close to the airport; it's just on the way.

Flipping on the blinker, he turns into the fast-food chicken place I've come to love. "Fil-A again? Drive-thru?"

"You're a keeper, Richardson. Drive-thru chicken is the best fake dinner date ever."

He laughs at my sarcasm. "I know you'd rather be looking for Madison than at a nice, sit-down dinner. I like this place too."

"See, this is why we get along so well. You know what I like and don't try to push places on me like my father would. He and my mother would be chiding me about unhealthy calories and being in the spotlight, while you tell me to order extra waffle fries."

"You're an adult and swim too much to be unhealthy."

I nod, completely agreeing. He orders my favorite sandwich, large ice water, extra fries, and a parfait for me then gets a cobb salad and extra chicken for himself. We pull through the drive-thru and then eat once we get in the parking lot of the strip club. BJ's Dollhouse flashes at us as we eat like it's the best thing we've had in days. That isn't the case, though. Richardson has been spoiling me every few days with Fil-A, so I've been eating well this entire trip.

He takes the lead, coming around to my door. I get out and stick close to his side. It's dark, and protocol is that I have more than one guard with me in the evenings. We're breaking that by giving the others a much-needed night off. The bouncer checks our ID's at the door and charges Richardson a fifteen-dollar cover charge. The bouncer reassures me that I get in for free since I'm a good-looking woman. I snort but refrain from rolling my eyes like I want to. I'm sure some women are flattered by the bouncer's words, but I take it at face value. More women in the place means more men, paying their cover charge and the dancers. It's not rocket science.

"Drink?" Richardson suggests as we find an empty table. The bar doesn't have many people here tonight. There are a few lonely guys scattered throughout with one other table occupied. The three guys sitting there jovially laughing and drinking are wearing leather jackets showing a creepy looking skull wearing a crown in the middle.

"Not yet. You sit here, and when the server comes over, ask about Madison, please. Maybe if they have any new strippers scheduled to dance, too. You know the drill."

"Okay, I can do that."

"I'm going to walk over to the bar and scan the liquor bottles to see what they have. I'll pass by that table over there, and if any of them speak to me, I'll ask about my sister."

"I don't like the idea of you going over there by yourself. They look like dangerous criminals, and your father would have my job. We're already going outside our regular procedure."

"This isn't our first recon, Richardson. You know that table would be more receptive if I walk by versus you asking them for information. We have to step outside our box to find my sister. Nothing has worked so far. My gut tells me that they may know something. I don't know why I get that feeling, but I have to go on it."

His lips part as he exhales, looking uncomfortable. "Fine, but if anything goes south, you know what to do."

I concur. "Head for the bathroom and stay there until you've neutralized the threat. Call for backup. Never put myself in harm's way, especially when you're neutralizing the possible threat."

"Good. Signal if you need me."

I flash a wide smile in case anyone's watching us and start laughing as I stand like we're not going over a routine exit strategy. We'd come up with this plan a long time ago when we realized my sister was hanging out at some rough places.

"Can I help you?" the bikini-clad bartender asks as I approach. I tap my chin as I gaze behind her, acting like the typical party girl about to go binge drinking. I went to college with many of them, so I know the look well, even if I never partook in their detrimental life decisions.

"Yes, can I please have a margarita on the rocks, but can you put it in that bigger glass?" I point to her Long Island tea glasses.

"It won't be very strong unless you want a double."

"If you'll fix it normal and then top it off with Sprite, that would be perfect."

Her brow raises, not impressed in the least bit with the changeup. Less alcohol means less money in her case.

I lean in. "I want my date to think I'm drinking, but still have my wits about me. You know, just in case. This is our first date."

"Ah, that's a neat trick and smart, to boot." She winks and goes about making my drink. She sets it on the bar, and as I go to dig out my cash, she holds her hand up. "It's on the house."

"Wow, thank you!"

"Ladies drink free as long as it's not something crazy. The boss doesn't like to advertise that, though. If we pretend that we're giving it to a pretty woman for free on the down low, then you're more likely to tell your friends."

Laughing, I nod. "I appreciate the honesty."

I grab the cup, taking a sip. It's the Sprited-down version of a margarita so I can do recon and not get tipsy. If I weren't looking for my sister, I'd have a top-shelf double margarita in a heartbeat, especially with Richardson watching my back. I love tequila, but unlike Madison, I don't indulge often. It's also a relief knowing I have Richardson around to watch over me if I feel the need to. He's not interested in me sexually, so I feel safe with him. I can drink without worrying I'll be unexpectedly taken advantage of by anyone meaning me ill will.

I'm headed back to our table when my hip brushes one of the biker's arms resting on the back of the plush chair. I pause, feigning shock, even though I did it on purpose. "Oh! I'm sorry about that, are you all right?" I ask, meeting his stern stare.

"Of course, I am, darlin'," he rumbles, and I glance to the patch on his breast.

"Plague?" I ask. "Wow, how'd you get that name?"

He chuckles, his dark features lighting as he buys into my act. "I like to party, and by the looks of it, so do you. Long Islands aren't for weak drinkers."

My smile grows, pleased that the big cup did the trick. "I like to call it my frog drink. It's loaded with more ta-kill-ya than anything." I wink to sell the lie better. Politics and acting go hand in hand, so it's no wonder I'm pulling this off with flying colors.

"I'll have to give that one a try sometime. Though I usually toss back tequila straight, no need to pussy around when you know what ya want." It leaves him rumbling with a growl, and I have no doubt in my mind that he's no longer talking about alcohol. This is where I have to be careful. It's okay to be friendly—a little flirty even—but if I lead this man on, I'm liable to be raped.

The other bikers' lips curl with amusement at my term for tequila. The two of them flash cautionary glances over at Richardson, seeing what he makes of this exchange. The oldest of the group speaks up. "You're trouble, sweetheart, aren't ya?" His green eyes sparkle, enjoying my attention on their group. He doesn't strike me as the mean type. The other two are a bit rougher around the edges, but this one doesn't project that. With the way he gazes over me fondly, I suspect he has a thing for younger women. He's probably pushing somewhere between fifty and fifty-five. I'm not usually drawn to men that much older than me, but he's extremely handsome.

"I mean, I could be, but it depends on who's asking." I giggle, offering him a wide smile. He doesn't want to hurt me, just have a good time. It's the other two that have me on edge. The guy in the middle—Blow, according to his patch—he's got that just fucked hairstyle, kind of a messy fauxhawk. He wears cocky arrogance all over his perfect features. His plump lips would no doubt be amazingly soft if they were to touch my body. That won't ever happen, but I can fantasize. It's the only safe option with him, as this guy screams bad boy.

"Oh, yeah? What brings you in tonight?" I check the flirty older guy's breast patch. Apparently, his name is Whiskey. Somehow it seems to fit, and I don't even know him. "You looking to party? We can make that happen. Drop the guy with the stick up his ass and call up a few friends."

I ignore the dig at my security and go for sweet. "I like your name, Whiskey," I compliment, and he flashes me teeth, pleased with my praise. I use that as my in to find out what I really want to know. "Actually, I'm already here looking for a friend of mine. Maybe you guys know her?"

"What's her name, baby?" Plague rumbles, drawing my eyes back to him. His irises are the color of melted dark chocolate. He has short black hair and tattoos peeking out everywhere—some even dot his face in various spots.

"Well, she's even crazier than I am. Uh, she kind of looks like me…her name is Madison."

The biker in the middle sits up, his back jolting straight and shoots a dark look at Whiskey. His tense response garners my attention. It's like a red flag and has me hoping she's not been hurt by them or anyone else.

I glance to his breast patch again, making sure I got his name right the first time before I ask outright, "Do you know her?" I meet Blow's hard glare straight on. My sister's whereabouts are too important to me to be intimidated by this biker.

He stares up at me for a beat before eventually growling. "I may know someone who does… Depends though, who the fuck are you?"

"Alice Compton, her sister."

Chapter 5

Doubting yourself is normal.
Letting it stop you is a choice.
- Mel Robbins

Ripper

Found the bitch sniffing around again. She's here. Right now.

I read the text from Blow three times before it clicks. He's talking about the woman from before. Alice, something or other. I can't remember the last name I wrote down, but her first has stuck with me.

Bring her to me. I text back, not giving a fuck if they have to knock her unconscious to get her here. I want to see this woman for myself and find out why she's so desperately searching for her sister. I'd understand if the chick was underage, but she's midtwenties, plenty grown to make her own damn decisions.

Whiskey texts me next. **Alice is at BJ's again.**

I know. Blow hit me up. Bring her to me.

He replies while Blow leaves me hanging. **She's got a man on her. Looks like a date, but I'd bet it's security.**

Bring the fucker along. I'll slit his throat myself if he attempts to step in.

Bet. His name shows up once more with the response, and I shove the phone back in my cut. I had our cuts special made, so we have inside pockets in all of them at our breast. It's an excellent spot to keep a bulletproof plate—or drugs—depending on where you're at. Most of us hold our license and cash in it, so we don't have to worry about bitches trying to be sneaky and jack us while we're getting fucked up.

I'm curious to meet this bitch and see what she's all about. Not often does a chick have the guts to go poking around strip clubs and talking to some rowdy looking bikers. It makes me believe she's got some balls on her, and that piques my curiosity. The brothers haven't exactly been forthcoming, so I need to check her out for myself.

I haven't had some good pussy since I was up north, stopping in on Gamble, so I'm sure that's fucking with my head as well. Gamble was patched as prez while visiting New Orleans, and once I caught word of her club giving her shit, I hit the road. That bitch went through a lot to have to deal with some mouthy motherfuckers pissed off that she has a pussy and the patch. I helped get them in line with her buddy Ghost while hitting some club whore gash and popped smoke back to Texas once I knew she'd be straight.

Maddy's been the only bitch around much since then, and I've only allowed her to suck my cock. Blow's been dipping into that pussy on the regular, so I've held back, letting him take her for a ride. Sure, we have other sweetbutts that try to squirm their way into our beds, but none of them stick out like fresh pussy does.

The brothers take their sweet-ass time. No doubt they're having a few more drinks while they know I'm at the club. I'm over here twiddling my fucking fingers, waiting on their asses. *Fuckers.* They went out to relax and shoot the shit while I stuck around and took care of business. Sure, being prez means I delegate a lot of shit, but I still take on a portion of tasks as well. I'm no lazy fucker, and I never will be.

I head for the bar, the prospects scurrying out of my way like frightened rats. Each brother has a prospect sponsored, aside from myself. I don't have time to hold anyone's hand in this world, so they have to do it. I just vet their choices in the end and either put them up for a vote or give 'em the boot to get the fuck out of my clubhouse. With the amount of MCs around this area, we need more numbers, whether I like it or not.

Ammo, Powerhouse's bitch boy, waits like an eager puppy for me to bark out, "Give me a beer."

I guess this clown knows his way around weapons. Not surprised since Powerhouse is the same way. Each of my brothers seemed to come up with prospects that're mini versions of themselves so far; it's been entertaining, to say the least, to witness it. If anything, I should be able to trust these green motherfuckers in the end, and that's what matters most in an outlaw motorcycle club. God knows if Rancid's fucked up ass ever showed his face around here to take me out, like he did with Dog in New Orleans, I need to have a club full of brothers watching my back. He's kept his cool with me in the past, but the way he works, you never know what to expect. He doesn't live by the same set of code most of us other prez's do. Considering he's the big dog, the prez of prez's, means no one can touch him for it either.

"Yes, Prez." Ammo moves like his ass is on fire, popping the top and handing it over.

I nod my gratitude and step outside.

Wrench, Whiskey's prospect, is in the garage with the bay up, clinking around in there. He's one hell of a mechanic. He'll get a patch eventually. He knows how to keep his fucking mouth shut and pitch in around here. He's always working on someone's bike or vehicle, whether it's his or not. I'd give him my vote today if it were his time. He's got another month or so of waiting around.

The other two dipshits are on patrol. Blow brought in a kid barely eighteen…kid's a sneaky-ass thief. We call him Mouse since he's so fucking quiet. You never know when the fucker's sneaking up on ya. He's the newest and has at least another year of prospecting before he's put up for a patch.

Plague sponsored a buddy of his—Manic. We call him that 'cause the fucker will party until he blacks out. Not only that but when he fights, he goes completely nuts, falls into a straight-up rampage. While he may be a liability, we can use a few fuckers around here with their screws loose. It gives us an edge that other clubs won't want to touch.

Angel, my enforcer who's currently out on a job, sponsored Lunatic. His name says it all and makes me question Angel's thinking. Those two would scalp every motherfucker who crosses them if I didn't put a stop to it. Bad enough they chop up damn near every kill. I don't know how they stomach the shit. They've bonded in ways I could never imagine with another human being. For women's sake, I hope no one is ever dumb enough to fall for either one of them. Lord knows one day they wouldn't wake up. Luna is with Angel now, but when they're home, he sleeps in the shop, away from the rest of the club. Angel doesn't want him under the clubhouse's roof until he's fully patched. Considering he's his sponsor, we've respected his wishes.

Hearing the telltale signs of multiple pipes headed my way, I turn around and head right back inside. I go straight to my office. I already have the upper hand bringing her to the RBMC clubhouse, but I'll get some much-wanted privacy in my office. I want to feel her out myself, find out exactly what she's up to, and if her words are genuine. That's easier to pick up on without multiple distractions happening around the club.

I'm also curious if her security guy is ballsy enough to step foot in here with her. I'm in a mood today, one where I wouldn't mind knocking some teeth out. Maybe he'll provoke me enough I'll get a chance to. That'd be fun and no doubt scare the shit out of this nosey bitch.

The club door slams a beat later, and my eyes go straight for the security cam I have mounted on the wall in my office. The yard out front is littered with bikes and two swanky black sedans. Apparently, she didn't ride with one of the brothers unless the dipshit she was with had followed her here. If that were the case, though, I know my brothers would've lost him, so Alice must've ridden here with him. That knowledge pisses me off. I told my brothers to bring her. What if she'd tried to get away once they were on their bikes? And who the hell does the other cage belong too? While she was doing God knows what with the brothers, dickmunch must've called for backup. What a chicken shit little weasel. I mean, it was in his best interest, but still, the pussy must not have any nuts between his legs.

Whiskey is first to duck into the spacious office, followed by Blow. I'm about to lay into them and ask where the fuck Plague slithered off to when the woman in question crosses the threshold to my office. She's flanked by three non-impressive bodyguards with Plague taking up the rear. At least he had enough sense not to walk in front of them. I swear, sometimes it's like I'm dealing with a group of fucking toddlers. You don't let your possible enemy behind you. That's Common Sense 101. At this rate, I may end up knocking some sense into my brothers instead of the dipshits she's brought with her.

"'Bout time you pussies showed up," I grumble instead to my guys, casting my glower to the fine piece of meat standing in front of my desk. I lay eyes on her, and she's hot enough to make my groin tighten with desire. Rarely do bitches have that power over me right away, and this one has me taking notice. That fire engine red dress she's got on is like waving a flag at a bull. I want to show her just how badly I can rip her in two.

So, she's related to Maddy the stripper, hmm? I can see the resemblance, but this one outshines the other, for sure.

Her three suits scan the area—for her safety, I'm assuming. Never mind, she couldn't be safer, surrounded by a group of motherfucking vipers. We're not some prep school trained bodyguards either. We're criminals, the low-ball kind that won't think twice about fighting dirty. We're callous and take no shit, so these guys have another thing coming if they believe they could protect her from *me*. I'm the worst one of them all. Those stick-up-their-ass motherfuckers barely flash a glance in my direction, acting like I don't exist. That shit irritates me the fuck off, not showing respect where it's due. People thinking they're better than me—always have—but this is my house, my club. They need to open their eyes and take notice who's top dog up in this motherfucker.

"Can I help you?" I ask, flicking my gaze over her from top to bottom. I could stare all day, she's that fuckin' fine. Bet she'd look even more desirable on her knees begging for my cock. She's got full, round tits that're asking for my dick to titty fuck 'em. Now, that'd damn sure be the proper way to get me to talk about her stripper sister.

"I hope so," she replies confidently. I don't know what I find more attractive on her right now, her big tits, or the fact she'll meet my intense stare and not falter. She's not submissive, which has always been an attractive trait on women for me.

"Mm," I grunt, noncommittal. I can't believe these fucking suits haven't said shit about the way I'm eyeing their master. If they could read my thoughts, however, I wonder if they'd act on it? Right now, I'd enjoy ripping that crimson dress right off this uppity bitch to fuck her on my desk in front of everyone.

"I'm searching for my sister. I was hoping you could tell me if you've seen her."

I crack a grin—not a friendly one. "What are you willing to give me for it?" I take pussy, drugs, and cash. I'm guessing she has two out of three to offer me.

She draws in a quick breath, her determination showing as her brow wrinkles. She doesn't take my bait. "This is a serious matter, I assure you. My sister has been gone for nearly two months now, and her family is extremely worried. I'm worried. Please be sensible about this and let me know if you've seen her." She holds out a photo to me. She's got clear gloss on her nails with white tips. They're nothing like the long bright nails I'm used to bitches raking over my back as I fuck them. I guess hers are long enough to make me feel them. We'll see.

I don't reach to take it, but instead, keep my eyes locked with hers. I want to stir up some shit, see how trained these jackasses really are. Her long-lost sister is the least of my issues, and she's gotta play to pay, but she doesn't seem to get that just yet. "That all you've got to offer me? Let me make this easy on you: I accept, pussy, drugs, and cash as payment."

"How much will it cost me to get you to look at the photo?" She's brazen I'll give her that, coming at me so boldly and not being an eager club whore. Clearly, she's used to having backup, 'cause most bitches will barely speak a peep when I come face-to-face with 'em unless it's to beg me to take their pussy or mouth. I can bark at them to *suck my cock,* and they drop to do as they're told. I have a feeling Alice would tell me no. That's one fuck of a challenge I can't simply pass up. I will get inside her pussy, no matter how long it takes me.

I shrug, my eyes crinkling with amusement. "Now we're getting somewhere, and I've changed my mind. I don't want money or drugs; I want your warm, wet cunt."

She gasps in outrage, and the bodyguard closest to her lunges for me. "Stop!" she yells suddenly, clenching onto the suit's arm. She stands between him and me.

I've merely stood from my chair, waiting for him to get close enough for me to hit.

"Please, Richardson," she soothes. "Th-this is important. They could be the key to finding Madison to us going home with my little sister."

"You don't deserve that kind of disrespect," he argues, still not casting a look in my direction.

The pansy-ass is whipped. I want to taunt his ass for it, but I wait to see if she'll take me up on my request. I won't force her to give it up. I've never had to, and I won't start that now. There are too many women out there giving gash up for free, to take it from one.

She agrees. "I know, but please, just let me handle this."

"Fine," he grits eventually, not liking it one bit. He steps back in his original spot like a good little soldier.

I chuckle. I can't help it. I'm a fucking dick and find this entirely too entertaining. My guys quietly wait for my next move. Whiskey perches on his desk while Blow and Plague chill against the wall on either side of our company. Right now, they're doing what they're supposed to and waiting for my lead. If I decide to hit someone, they'll make sure to have my back.

She faces me again, her beauty making me swear under my breath. Fuck, this woman is on another level entirely when it comes to the ass I see on the regular. "Please."

Exhaling a sigh, I rub the back of my neck. I want to get her flustered into giving me what I want, but I need to get her alone. Right now, she has these imbeciles to lean on, and I need to change that up. I murmur, going for a less confrontational approach, "You want me to look? Then take a walk with me."

"Okay, I can do that," she readily agrees, taking a step back as I stand once more and come around my desk. Her guys shuffle to the side to let me pass. It's smart on their part. I wouldn't hesitate to move them out of my way myself.

"Alone!" I hiss when the guards seem to think they're coming with us.

"Ma'am, this is against protocol." One of the other suits finally speaks up, his anxiety making itself known. I'm guessing the first guy is her lead, and these two jokers are bodies taking orders. "Your father wouldn't approve."

Her temper flares at his proclamation, a blush peppering her cheeks and neck. She exhales, no doubt counting to ten to keep up this unruffled façade of hers. "Thank you for your concern, but I'm an adult. You guys will be right here if I need anything. I'm assuming you're trained enough to get to me, or was my father mistaken when he hired you?" She throws down the passive-aggressive gauntlet, and I commend her on it. It's sexy as fuck to see her call off her leashed dogs for me.

I hold out my elbow to her, pushing the boundaries a touch further. Surprisingly, she steps closer and takes my offering. Her tender touch has my biceps flexing, and I mutter, a bit breathless at the tingle her skin elicits on mine, "This way." I lead her out of my office and through the back door. We make our way over the backyard to eventually stop at the fire pit. I tip my head at one of the lawn chairs, and she sits. I take the stump next to her, my legs spreading immediately to make room for my heavy dick. She has me on the very edge of being hard. My jeans are squeezing the fuck out of me, my cock reminding me that I need to get laid and badly.

"You enjoy stirring up trouble, don't you?" she asks a moment later. It's not chastising, only curious. I like her out here, like this—alone and mine for the taking. It's semi late, the sky dark with a spring chill in the air. The club has several lights on out here so I can see her without any issues.

"It has a certain appeal." I shrug.

"So... uh, what's your name?" She tries to break the ice, though the patch on my breast says it boldly. Maybe she can't see well at night, so I let it go.

"Ripper."

"Ripper, now that I've done as you've requested, would you please take a look at the photo of my sister?"

I crack my neck, running my palms over my jean-clad thighs. "She must mean a lot if you'd chance coming into a place like this. It's damn near the middle of the night, and you're around dangerous men, yet you keep hounding me over her."

"Sorry to burst your bubble, but you don't intimidate me, Mr. Ripper. I understand that this is your life, your business. I respect that. I'm simply asking for your help. I figure it never hurts to ask. If you say no, then I have to accept that and leave. I've done what I can, and I have to keep up my search elsewhere."

"You're telling me that I don't scare you, even just a little? I could break your frail neck with only my hands." I widen them, holding my hands out that could easily palm a basketball to get my point across. She's so delicate and I'm tatted up, rough and rowdy, used to working for everything I want. When I say work, I don't necessarily mean the legal way either. I pour a bit of fire starter on the pit, lighting it with a long match. We keep them out here in a plastic bag, so they don't get ruined. I need the warmth. I wasn't made for winter or cold weather. It'll also offer up some more light, so I can read her expressions better.

"Many men could, I suppose, but I don't know…something tells me you won't hurt me out here." She gestures around us.

I nod, conceding. "You're right. I won't hurt you like that, not ever. I don't make it a habit to hurt women." It makes me sick, to be honest, to know that some take advantage of the fact we're physically stronger in most cases when it comes to females. "Those who betray me and mine…that's another story, however."

"Thank you," she breathes out. Her shoulders drop with it, releasing some of the tension they'd held when we started walking.

"Tell me about yourself." I take in her unrelenting beauty once more. She may not seem like much in her father's uppity world filled with plastic surgery, but in mine, she's a diamond—a natural beauty.

"Will this help me find Madison?"

I shrug noncommittally. "Maybe. I'm a biker, babe. I don't offer up information to everyone when they ask. That'd be too easy. You want something from me, you gotta give me something in return, that's how all this works. Tell me who you are, why you're worried about your sister…the truth, and if I'm willing, then I'll see if I know anything about this missing Maddy."

Her eyes flair at her sister's nickname, and it's like the floodgates have been opened. Alice knows damn well that I have information on her sister. She's far too smart for her own good, especially if it leads her down dark roads like it did tonight. She'd probably flip out if she was aware that the woman in question was at her own place, wherever that may be, cleaning up. Maddy will be back here soon enough, no doubt, eager to hop on my brother's dick and ride him into oblivion. Blow went to the bar. She could've gone with him, but she chose to use the time to regroup for him. Maddy doesn't have any clue how lucky she got; that's for sure.

Alice talks for hours, sitting back in her lawn chair in front of the fire. She tells me anything and everything I ask of her. She's single, the oldest, and used to be a champion swimmer. With each new detail, I become a little more infatuated with her. My brothers had given me all the information on her they could find, but it's nothing compared to hearing it straight from the horse's mouth.

Her spiel makes me want to keep her here with me. Although I know if I do that, then her senator daddy will come searching for her, guns blazing. The last thing I need to be caught up in the middle of a media frenzy with the senator of some state up north is the Royal Bastards MC.

If Rancid, the OG prez from the first chapter, caught wind of it, I'd be fucked. He'd be foaming at the mouth to have me taken out and gain the ability to place someone else in my spot. He was already irritated that I stepped in for Gamble and suggested she take a prez spot in another club, rather than continue to be treated like his personal whore. I had to, though. He would've ended up killing her, and that sweet woman didn't deserve such a twisted fate. No way would my brothers allow any harm to come to me from Rancid's threats if this whole thing went south, and it'd turn bloody—quick. My brothers would die for me, and I won't put them in that position unless it's absolutely necessary.

I amp up the fire as time passes us by. In Texas, the spring nights can still run a little chilly. She took me up on a beer earlier, and as the minutes pass, she becomes more accessible in my eyes. Reaching over, I tuck a strand of hair behind her ear. I desperately want to kiss her, but I hold back. I know now, after spending time with her, that she doesn't like being bullied into something. That's my usual MO for getting shit handled, but Alice is different, and she makes me want to act inversely with her. Maybe if things keep up as they are, I can coax a taste of her lips. Regardless, I'll have that kiss before she leaves tonight. That, I'm damn sure of. She has to leave here with my taste on her lips. She needs to think of me afterward, so her fine ass comes back again.

"Your hair's lighter than hers," I find myself noting aloud as the flames flicker and pick up on the hues in her hair. I also can't help but want to keep her interested.

"So, you do know her..."

"Hm," I grunt, not sure how much I should let on. "Let's just say, I'm aware of who you're talking about. *Knowing her* wouldn't be the term I'd use, though." Maddy knows my cock, however.

"Please, tell me. Was she here?" she rushes out, glancing around to finally stop on the illuminated clubhouse. Knowing Blow, Maddy is probably inside with him now, snorting a few lines. They're probably getting ready to have their own private party with just the two of them.

"It's going to take more than you sitting here for a few hours for me to talk, Gem."

She meets my stony stare. "But you said if I opened up, you'd tell me about Madison."

"And I kept my side of the deal. I acknowledged that I know of her," I reason.

Her bottom lip trembles. I don't think she's going to cry, though. It seems more from outrage. She sinks her teeth into it, and it draws me in closer. She has no idea how alluring she is. Like a moth to a flame, I'm drawn to her.

My lips lightly brush against hers, nearly to the point you'd swear it didn't even happen. I whisper against her lips, allowing her to taste a hint of my words, to sample the Jack I'd thrown back earlier. "How bad do you want it? The information? What will you *do* for it?"

She admits, "Whatever I have to. I'll do whatever it takes."

A groan escapes me before my hand moves to the back of her head, and I dive in. I suck her plump bottom lip between mine, nibbling and coaxing her mouth to part for me. Once she allows it, my tongue slips inside, tangling with hers. She doesn't follow or hide away, but rather, meets me head-on. Our mouths fight for dominance, and it's one of the most erotic experiences I've felt with a stranger. This woman makes me want to consume her and drown in her every whim.

Her hands move to my chest, fisting my cut in her grip as she holds on. She's rooted in place as our lips come together, feeling the others out. This woman was made for me, the kiss alone has thoughts whispering in my mind to strip her this very second and fuck her. My caveman instinct tells me to lock her away and claim her before anyone else has the chance. I could own her, fuck her until she relents and calls me her ruler. Those thoughts spiral through my head as we selfishly ravage one another until the spell's broken. I'm left hot, my blood boiling in my veins for her, wanting more.

"Ma'am." A throat clears, and I let loose a savage roar to the fuck stick who interrupted us. His eyes widen, but he holds his ground, a few feet away from us. He silently watches as Alice backs away, releasing her hold to smooth the thick leather under her palms. Her breath comes in soft, heated pants as we part, our stares locked on one another. I could rip that motherfucker in two for ruining such a perfect moment.

Alice clears her throat, throwing a brief glance at the dickweed. She nods, telling me, "I need to go. It's getting late, and my father will be expecting me to call first thing to relay what I've found out so far."

"You want to know more, you'll come back." I drive the point home with a stern glare at her and the jackass who's too close for my liking. She better fucking come back. She's got me hooked already, and I'll hunt her ass down if I have to. One thing's for sure, she and I aren't finished yet.

"Promise me," she demands right back.

I let loose a snort and bark, "Fuck promises."

Alice murmurs, "If you want me to come back, you will promise me."

The woman is going to be my undoing. I want nothing more than for her to return and give me more time, a chance to sink deep into that little cunt of hers. "Fine," I relent, my voice gruff with irritation and pent up desire. My palm slides away from her hair, landing on my thigh. "I should take you home."

"On the back of your motorcycle?" she asks.

I shrug it off like it's nothing. Although, it's a pretty big fucking deal for me to offer.

"Maybe another time, but thank you."

I nod and stand, holding my hand to help her up. She takes it, adopting a beautiful smile in response. I mutter, "My brothers will leave you alone. I'll make sure they don't fuck with you…if you come back, that is."

"I appreciate that, Ripper. I can assure you, I'll be seeing you soon."

I don't say anything else as we walk toward the club. There's nothing for me to say. She might come back, she might not. In my lifestyle, chicks like her rarely double back, so I won't hold my breath. Doesn't mean I won't hunt her fine ass down, though. Some people wait for fate to take control, but in her case, I'll make fate happen when I want it to.

"Later, Gem. Take care of yourself, yeah?" I say once we're at the back door. Her other dipshit guards are hovering by it like distressed parents on prom night.

"Gem?" she pauses to ask.

I nod. "You're a motherfuckin' diamond around here. A rare one."

Alice blushes and leaves. I hate to see her go, but damn, what a fine ass she has.

Chapter 6

*Focus on the step in front of you,
not the whole staircase.
- Homebody Club*

Church

"You gonna fill us in, Prez, on who that was the other day?" Powerhouse raises his brows, calling me out. It's cool; I'd be fuck all if these guys didn't keep me on my toes all the time and hold me accountable. Of course, he'd notice Alice and that big commotion I put on the other night when the brothers got her to the club. She's far too fucking sexy not to pay attention to—that much I know for sure.

"This isn't church business, fucker. You could've asked me when you saw them the other night." He's askin' about Alice because of Maddy. I know it. He probably saw the resemblance, and it has him thinking.

He grunts, looking to Blow.

"What?" I bark. "Blow, you gossiping like a bitch about me, brother?"

He shakes his head and huffs. "Fuck off me, bro. House came to me, and I told him it had to do with the strippers."

"Ah." My knuckles rap on the thick wood table before us. "Explains it, then. No wonder Powerhouse is being nosey." I meet my brother's gaze, seeing the concern for what it is now. "Your bitches are safe, brother. The club is straight. Old man BJ ain't got shit to worry his flaccid dick over."

His jaw unclenches, and he nods—grateful for me setting him at ease. He's like a motherfucking junkyard dog when it comes to those damn dancers. "Good. Who was she, then? And who were the suits? Those were the same johns I was telling you about before. They'd been around the strip club but didn't cause a stir. I thought they were just passing through."

Blow snaps his fingers. "That's right! Those were the same fuckers nosin' around, asking questions. I thought they were familiar but couldn't place them, but you nailed it."

Whiskey interrupts, a bit of sarcasm coating his tone. "Prolly 'cause you were tweaking. You've never been good with descriptions when you've been snorting product." He taps the side of his head. "Gotta stop burning up all those brain cells, kid."

Blow shrugs. "Have to escape the bullshit somehow, brother."

We leave it alone after that. Ain't none of us trying to dig into Blow's demons. That's his shit to live with.

"She came here for Maddy." I finally fill everyone in, though I'm sure they've already guessed, for the most part. "Alice is her older sister, and the pack following her around was her bodyguards."

Plague lets out a low whistle. "Must be *somebody*, if she's got private security."

I take a swallow of beer before continuing. "Their father is Senator Compton."

The brothers gaze at me, lost. None of them have any idea who the fuck stick is. I didn't realize it either until I thought long and hard on it.

I continue. "He's nothing to Texas. No surprise you haven't heard of him. He's making waves in the Midwestern area. The name only clicked with me because I rode up to see Gamble. I'd passed a shit ton of political signs and that motherfucker was painted over most of them."

"Fuck!" Blow yanks at his hair. He realizes that he's been in bed with a senator's daughter. Not only fucking her but feeding her copious amounts of drugs, and this could fall back on him to bite him in the ass.

"Sounds about right." I flash him a glance, nodding my agreement. "Alice is in town searching for Maddy. According to her, little sister likes to up and run on occasion, and this is nothing new for their family. Alice was sent by their father to bring Maddy home before she ended up in some real trouble. Maddy's managed to stay under their radar for longer than usual, so the old man's losing his shit. Understandable, considering it's his daughter and all."

Whiskey complains, "This could bring heat on the club—motherfuckin' bad heat."

Plague bobs his head, keeping whatever thoughts he has on it to himself.

"She assures me that her father wants to keep all this as quiet as we do. He's one of the few senators without a public scandal tainting his name, so he flips over this shit apparently."

"Well, fuck, that's good news," Whiskey retorts, massaging his temples.

"Stop being so fucking dramatic, old man." I roll my eyes in Whiskey's direction and continue. "He's also willing to pay for Maddy's return."

Powerhouse kicks out a grin. "This could benefit us," he remarks. Our club enjoys a free payday, and, in this case, it practically fell in our laps.

I grunt. *It could, but do I want to take advantage of Alice? I'd rather see her. We already have money coming in regularly.*

"Surely, you're not gonna pass this up?" he goads.

"We can vote on it," I finally concede. When it comes to money, it involves all of us, whether I wanna like it or not. "Nays?" I ask, and Blow signals with me, unsurprisingly. "Ayes?" I don't need to ask, but it's protocol.

Powerhouse, Whiskey, and Plague gesture for the payday. "That settles it, then. We offer up Maddy for cash in hand."

"Fucking bullshit," Blow hisses.

I cut him a glare. "Club law, motherfucker. Shut up." Hell, I voted with him, but this is the way of our brotherhood, and it's worked for us so far.

Whiskey clears his throat. "I'd like to bring something to the table."

"Yeah?" I nod him on to proceed.

"Wrench has paid his dues as a prospect. I'd like to vote on making him a full member...with your approval, of course, Prez."

"Figured it'd be coming up. If you'd brought it to the table sooner, I'd have agreed too. Wrench pulls his weight for the club, in my opinion. How do you feel, brothers?"

"Let's fucking vote." Blow backs me up, his head in club mode once again.

"All right. Those in favor of Wrench being patched and brought into the fold?"

The table echoes with our *ayes*, and it's quickly settled. He not only gains full membership now and his rockers, but a paycheck from the club to boot. We split up our paydays for club expenses, and anything left over is divvied up between the patched members.

"Whiskey, you were his sponsor, so take care of his patches and whatnot. We'll celebrate once you have 'em."

"Angel getting back any time soon?" Powerhouse asks. Angel is our club enforcer; he got his road name from the *angel of death*. Powerhouse has been filling the role of enforcer in the club while our brother's been gone. He's our sergeant at arms, so he's used to dealing with shit for us, regardless. The club feels the loss of not having Angel around. The dark motherfucker has a finesse about him and his distorted ideas of handling club threats.

I shrug. "The other charter needed him. He'll be back when he's finished helping their enforcer. You know how it is, brothers. We can never have too many favors owed to us."

Blow smirks. "Kinda like you riding up to the other charter to help out ol' Gamble?"

This asshole thinks I've got it bad for Gamble. He doesn't realize that just because Gamble has a pussy, it doesn't mean I want to fuck her or have already in the past. "I've said it before, we're cool. I rode up because if it were me taking over a club, I'd want the other charters to step in and have my motherfuckin' back. I have hers. Would she come if I called in need? That's to be seen. I'd like to think so, but don't plan on ever needing her to."

"Bet," Plague comments. "Well, on the business side, I've had everyone come through. I hit that trailer park on the far end of town, and the tweakers came out of the woodwork like cockroaches. Sold my stash in two days."

"The cocaine business is booming, brothers." I flash a wide smile. "We keep having paydays like we've had lately, and we'll need to recruit even more so. Whiskey, work on a new pledge, and if Wrench has any possible prospects in mind, he needs to talk it over with Blow. We're close to Oath Keepers territory, and if they catch wind of us dealing and expanding, it'll be war. Their clubs are too big for us to fuck with, without calling in any backup of our own. Keep your dealings on the down-low, and we'll milk this senator for whatever we can get out of him."

By the end of church, everyone's content. I know Blow isn't anticipating us selling out his latest fuck toy, but at the end of the day, that's all she is. We've each sacrificed for the club in some way, so him offering up a piece of ass shouldn't be a big deal. "We straight then? Anything else we need to discuss?"

The brothers grunt out various nos.

I take another pull from my beer and rumble out, "Dismissed!"

"When do you see Alice again?" Blow questions once the other brothers have left church, and it's just us two hanging back.

"Don't know." I shrug. Wish I did, though. Sure would make my thoughts about her chill the fuck out.

"You're telling me you haven't spoken to her? How do you know this senator thing is a go?"

I get to my feet, and he follows suit. "I dangled the very thing she desires in front of her. I hinted at knowing where her sister was and gave up a few details that don't mean a damn thing. At first, I wasn't sure she'd return, but she texted me the next day, telling me again that she'd be back. I knew if I put my number in her phone, she wouldn't be able to resist. Bitches like her crave control far too badly to let me be a possible lead and slip away."

"But she hasn't shown up yet?"

"Alice is smart. I think she's biding her time to see how eager I am. If I reach out, she knows she's got me hook, line, sinker. If I bide *my* time and let her come to *me*, we've got the ace in hand."

"Damn, Prez, that's deep." He grins.

I chuckle. We've been friends for far too long for me not to laugh when he gives me shit. "Shut up, fucker. Let's break out the Jack."

We head for the bar. I don't tell him that I'm hoping the whiskey will help drown out my thoughts of Alice. The bitch has been on my mind ever since she walked in my door, and I got a good look at her.

Taking a hefty swig of the potent liquor, I change the subject. "Tell Maddy to take off her clothes and come dance for us."

His grin grows. "Now that sounds like a good fuckin' time. I'll see what I can do." He walks off, and I can't help but wonder what ol' straitlaced Alice would think if she saw how we get down at the club when we want to party. She'd lose her shit if she discovered that most of the time, we end our parties without our clothes on. The Royal Bastards always end up fucking or getting our cocks sucked. It's one of the perks of being some of the baddest motherfuckers around.

I toss back the Jack. Even through the slight tingling burn of it, Alice is still right there on my mind, front and center. I sure do hope I get to fuck her by the time this is all said and done. The little meeting we had was a fucked-up version of foreplay for me, and it's only made me desire her more than before.

Plague tokes up, watching me flick a beer cap into the barrel we have at the end of the bar. We're filling it up to have a beer cap flag made. A couple of the brothers around here are good about creating cool, custom shit like that. Plague exhales a puff of smoke before asking, "Any update on Baker, Prez? Forgot to ask when we were in church last week."

Casting a glance in his direction, I shake my head. "Same ol' shit, brother. They're trying to make an example of him. He's still looking at serving a hundred-eighty days to two years; the DA hasn't backed off. If he's lucky, he'll be locked up in Hughes. At least if he's stuck in Gatesville, we can keep him protected. If he's sent to Beeville or Huntsville, it'll cost us to keep him alive."

"Christ…I thought Governor Abbott was supposed to be lightening up on possession charges of bud?"

"Mm." I nod. "Unless you're MC or gang-affiliated, then they're running you through the dirt. It's why we have to be more vigilant than ever when doing our runs or getting searched. They catch us with anything more than a joint, we're looking at a fight to stay out of lockup."

"That's some bullshit. Baker never fucks with anyone. He doesn't deserve this." He's right. Baker is one of the most levelheaded, chill dudes in the club. He got his road name because he's always baking something up laced with marijuana. He doesn't like to smoke the shit, but he damn sure likes to snack on it.

"Agreed, brother, but unless you can find a way to get on the DA's good side, then ain't fuck all changing for us...or Baker."

I chug the rest of my beer and toss it into the bin we have reserved for glass. I know what you're thinking, and just cause we're bikers doesn't mean we can't recycle. We drink a lot, so it only makes sense we make a haul of glass and cans to the recycling center every now and then.

Whiskey grumbles, throwing in, "I just checked up on our brother. He's holding up. Bitchy as ever, but he's managing. The money we've been throwing at county has kept the jailers off his back."

"Bet." Plague nods.

"We need to get him the fuck outta there; it's draining his cut of the pie, and I hate to see the brother get out to be left on his ass. You feel me?"

Whiskey agrees. "We're family. We have his back."

"Truth...this club has all our backs. Doesn't mean we can't acknowledge that being locked up is bad for business, and fuck if the other charters don't have their own shit hitting the fan."

"We'll figure it out," Whiskey declares stubbornly. At times, the older man has been a rock to me. I've known him damn near my entire life. He and my ol' man were close when I was a kid. My pops is in the life—not this club, but another. He and Whiskey met up when the clubs came together on a run back when I was six or so, and they'd remained friends ever since. While my father would never be in the Royal Bastards, I'm glad Whiskey had wanted in when his old club went their separate ways. It's not often a club just breaks down and separates like his did, but it allowed him to pledge to another set of colors.

"House!" Blow hollers out behind us, garnering our attention. We spin around wearing wry grins. Blow is always up to some shit with Powerhouse. Those two are like twelve-year-old BFFs joined at the hip at times—often getting into some sort of shit together.

I let out a snort at the sight before me. Powerhouse is naked save for material tied at his hip. It looks like they ripped up a sheet or some shit. He's wearing black, white, and red body paint. The brother looks like a fucking painted up goofball.

"The fuck is this shit?" Whiskey calls as the brothers and prospects hoot and holler loudly at our massive SAA who's got everything except his cock out on display.

He starts chanting some shit with Blow joining in, and we're all busting up. They stomp their feet, staying in the moment, both wearing surprised looks at us cutting up over the display. I have to put a stop to this nonsense. I hold my hand up, "You two fuck sticks want to explain what's happening?" I can barely ask with a straight face, gasping for air from laughing so hard. Obviously, these brothers have been cooped up too long to get them to start up shit like this.

It could be worse, I guess. They could be trying to kill each other.

Powerhouse stops, resting his hands on his hips, frowning at the room. His muscles flex, having been warmed up from his little stomp dance he'd just put on for us.

Blow shares, "We were looking at intimidation tactics. Figured we needed to come up with something good for House's next fight since he was called out. The videos said the symbols were protection and a sign of strength. We wanted to show it off before doing it at the fight."

"Un-fucking-believable," Whiskey complains, shaking his head. "Bunch of goddamn kids around here."

I start yelling in disbelief. "You're motherfucking bikers! Powerhouse, you're bigger than every fucker in here, and that's your intimidation tactic, brother? Christ, you two need to find a fucking hobby that doesn't include snorting the product and watching videos of this shit." The guys still chuckle in the background. Quietly, of course, or I'd be calling them out too.

Powerhouse stomps off, acting like a bitch who just got grounded. Hopefully, the sensitive fucker went to shower that shit off himself. Blow rolls his eyes and plops down in a chair. They remind me of chastised kids—the crazy fuckers.

"This is why I don't do drugs," Whiskey points out after a minute of silence.

"This is why I do drugs," Plague counters.

I chuckle. "This club is crazy, plain and simple. Maybe it's good Angel is away. He'd have decked both those idiots for pulling some shit like that."

The guys around me laugh. "That'd been entertaining," one of them coughs out as a chime echoes through the clubhouse.

"Someone's here," I growl, getting to my feet. I make my way to the monitor behind the bar to see Ammo and Mouse on either side of a black sedan outside at our gate. The cage's windows are tinted, and I immediately recognize the luxury brand. It took her ass a motherfuckin' week to show her face around here again. I can't believe what I'm seeing.

"All good?" Blow's instantly behind me, suddenly serious with the announcement of company. He fucks off a lot, but he's a decent VP when it counts. He straightens his shirt and snaps the buttons closed on his cut. "Anything I need to take care of?"

"It's her…"

"Maddy's sister?" he asks, craning his neck to see around me.

"Yep," I retort as my cell lights up. I press accept before it has a chance to ring. "How many are rolling with her?" I bark into the phone before the prospect can utter a word.

Mouse quietly replies, "She's, uh, got a carload, Prez. Two in the back, one driving, and her."

Guess they left the other car at home. Wonder why that is. I'll have to find out once I get her to myself again. "Fine, let them through. Oh, and Mouse?"

"Yeah, Prez?"

"You pat those motherfuckers down, but don't touch the woman."

"You're not afraid she's carrying too?"

"Did I fuckin' stutter, kid?"

"I hear you loud and clear. I'll take care of it."

"Bet," I hiss and tuck the phone away, my eyes still glued to the security screen. I shout, "Incoming, four bodies on the way. Pull your heads out of your asses."

The drinks get slammed down, the bottles cleared away. Everyone's back on alert. Powerhouse and Blow's little sideshow is put out of everyone's minds. I thoroughly enjoy shooting the shit and kicking back with my brothers, but business is business. As long as we have a potential payday from this senator, we need to be on our toes. There's also the small detail that I'm not one hundred percent sure how to take this confident chick. She's like a magnet, pulling me to her. That both enthralls and terrifies me.

Chapter 7

> Honestly, I don't need someone who sees the good in me. I need someone who sees the bad in me and still wants me.
> - Relationship Rules

Alice

"You came back," the president of the Royal Bastards MC greets me when I step into the bar. I wasn't sure if I was going to make it through the door as my detail weren't giving up their sidearms. I'd expect the smells of beer and sweat to hit me as I entered, but rather, it smells faintly of lemon and bleach, the same as the last time I was here. It's not spotless or anything—far from it—but it's straightened up for being a place full of men. Ripper looks just like I remembered, only he'd looked a bit disheveled last time. I'm here much earlier in the day, so he's very much put together.

I cast a glance around the room since it's brightly lit up this time around. The walls are littered with framed mugshots, along with random four by six snapshots pinned wherever they seem to fit. The ceiling is different yet intriguing. It's decorated in a mismatch of scuffed up hubcaps. Behind the fourteen-foot long hammered metal bar, the shelves are made out of iron bars and darkly stained wood. It screams rustic male in every aspect. I have to commend them. I've seen my father's friends hire decorators attempting to get a similar look and got nowhere near what the Royal Bastards have so effortlessly pulled off. There's an impressive Royal Bastards symbol painted on the far wall leading to Ripper's office that must have taken patience to craft.

There's no mistaking what this place represents or who fills it.

I flash Ripper a polite smile and tilt my head in acknowledgment. "I try to remain good on my word."

There's tension rolling around from every direction. I'm not sure whose is worse—the bikers or my bodyguards. I was hoping it wouldn't be as strained as my last visit, but apparently, that's asking for too much. I understand that both groups are weary coming from opposite ends of the spectrum, but this has to work so I can get the information I need. Madison must come first.

"I respect that." He holds his hand out.

I don't know what propels me to do so or why I feel comfortable around the hardened biker, but I do. I eagerly take his offered palm—his skin is rough with callouses. He easily tugs me closer...not that I mind. He has a charm about him that I'm sure is only directed toward women; otherwise, he's the epitome of his club name. Royal Bastard fits him handsomely, and I'm sure others before me agree. I have no doubt in my mind that if I were male, our previous interaction would've gone completely different, and I wouldn't be here now.

"Are we going for another walk?" I question, not sure how much alone time I can handle with him. His cocky attitude is appealing for some reason. I'd always been irked by people who act like he does, yet here I am, a fly caught in his trap. He's like opening a new book. I'm intrigued and want to gorge myself.

His lips tilt into a grin. He does that a lot, I remember from the last time. "Depends...you gonna let me have that pussy yet?"

I see he's back to his amiable smug self. I thought we'd gotten past that last week when we'd spoken for a few hours. He'd seemed more down-to-earth and less showy. Maybe it was the late night that'd calmed him down, and this is his usual self? I'd never dreamed of allowing anyone to speak to me this way, and he's no exception. I'd always imagined I'd slap a man if those words came out of his mouth, but these men aren't the type you slap and live to tell about it. I won't lie to myself and try to pretend that his attention doesn't fluster me either. I'm used to everyone minding their words around my family and me, and his crassness is bold and a bit refreshing.

Richardson wasn't quiet about it when we left last time either. He was fuming the entire car ride back. I could hear him plain as day screaming at his team on the other side of my hotel wall when we were supposedly all going to bed. He was incensed and insanely offended that Ripper took any kind of liberties with me. As far as I'm concerned, I have to deal with some discomfort if I'm going to find my sister. It's not like I've enjoyed visiting the dozens of strip clubs in search of her in the past or the men's leering looks that come along with it. Ripper making comments and touching me wasn't nearly as bad as Richardson had made it out to be. I'd be lying if I said I didn't appreciate at least a little of the attention from such a good-looking man. Ripper is powerful, like my own father, only in a different respect, and I can deny it all I want to, but it's alluring.

"I wouldn't hold my breath if I were you," I remark dryly, and he chuckles, amused with my banter. I walk beside him as he leads me through the club. My detail attempts to follow, but they're met with a wall of muscled bikers. It's no wonder Ripper acts as if he's untouchable; around his brothers, he is.

"Alice," Richardson calls, and I can hear the uneasiness coating his voice. He was completely against me returning to the biker compound. It's part of the reason it took me so long to make it back. I had to reassure my father multiple times that I wasn't in any danger around the Royal

Bastard's president. He wasn't easily convinced, but me finding Madison was higher on his list than a potential safety threat. I'd like to believe it was for Madison's welfare, but I'm not that naïve. I'm well aware it's my father's campaign outcome that's been weighing heavily on his mind.

"I'm okay," I assure Richardson and attempt to steal away Ripper's stern gaze he has pinned on my bodyguard. "Right?" I ask the man in question, squeezing the burly biker's hand where it's warming mine.

His hazel orbs meet mine, the anger fading away as he takes me in. He replaces it with a softer glance, one that promises me I'm safe with him. He looked at me the same way the night I was with him. "I won't hurt you...you have my word."

"See?" I send a pointed look at my guard. I catch him rolling his eyes, stewing at being told to calm down. "And no one else will hurt me while I'm with you, either, right?"

Ripper snarls at my suggestion. "It's not an easy feat to get through me, but I dare a motherfucker to try."

Oh, wow. Chills cover my body, sending a jolt of pleasure at his blatant display of alpha. *What is wrong with me? I shouldn't be turned on by all of this!* My core clenches, and I swallow tightly, wishing the zing between my thighs would stop.

My other guards' eyes widen, staring down Richardson. They're waiting for their lead to give them the order to take me out of here, away from Ripper. I'm not sure what good it'll do. The bikers at the gate took sidearms, and while my team is trained in hand-to-hand combat, these bikers are loaded with weapons. It wouldn't be pretty, that much I know, and it's the last thing I want to happen. I'm all for keeping the peace and not fighting.

I speak up before Richardson can stir up anything else. "It's fine, really. We discussed this already, and you can get to me if I need you." I pinch my ear, signaling the mic, and essentially telling them to remember the plan we have. If I need them, I'll say the code word, and they can jump in to rescue me like they're so handsomely paid to do.

Ripper completely ignores them after that and steers me around, heading for the back door. "Weather's too damn good in Texas right now to have you cooped up in my office. Unless you'd like to go to my room?"

"Ha-ha, no bedrooms," I reply sarcastically, and his chest rumbles with an amused chuckle. He may be all rough and tough, but he doesn't hesitate to laugh or smile. Maybe that's why I feel at ease being alone with him. I can't imagine a guy who wanted to hurt me would naturally act the way he does with me.

"Can't blame a brother for trying. Hell, if I didn't, I'd be just plain stupid."

We make it to the back, out by the fire pit again. He moves to sit on the biggest stump. Rather than release my hand, he tugs me to sit on his lap. I try to spring free, but he holds firm, his strength even more apparent in the awkward position.

"I'm not sitting on your lap."

"Mm, looks like you are to me."

"Not willingly," I sniff, playing the part of the perturbed female.

He snorts, not buying it. "I have no doubt in my mind that if you really wanted up, you could make it happen." Ripper grabs my hand, folding it until the heel is pushed out more than the rest. "You ever need to, you hit someone in the nose with this." He lightly taps the heel. "It'll get 'em to release you really quick. Give you enough of a chance to run." He ends his lesson with a wink, and my belly flutters with his sweetness in taking the time. He doesn't need to help me feel safe, yet he does so anyhow.

I'm trained in necessary self-defense, including a way to escape his hold, but he doesn't know that. Rather than admit he's called my bluff, I relax into his grasp. Maybe I don't really want him to let me go, but I feel like it's the right thing to do to ask him to let me up. I'm in the middle of Texas, alone, and still doing what I believe is expected of me. Fighting him won't lead me to my sister. I have to remember that, above all else.

"This isn't normal weather?" I go for a subject change, gesturing to the bright, sunny sky. I've never seen such beautiful weather during this time of year. Where I'm from, it's still pretty chilly, and you'd freeze at night without a jacket on.

"Hell, no. This is Texas. It's hot at least seven months of the year. The other five is bipolar; you never know what to expect."

I grin. "Bipolar weather, huh? I thought every state said that."

He shrugs. "Fuck if I know. I pay attention to my state. If we're on a run, then my brothers pay attention to that other shit. Part of the benefit of being prez." His brow raises, and I find myself smiling wider. I feel all giddy inside being this close to him, and that's a dangerous sensation. "How you been, Gem?" he finally asks, tilting his head to the side all cute like. He says the question in such a way that it's like he genuinely wants to know; he's not trying to make small talk for the hell of it.

"Is that what you really want to know?" I retort, a bit flirty, and he bites down on his bottom lip. If I weren't paying this close attention to him, I'd have missed the move. I wonder if I shake him up inside the way he does me?

"Nah, I want to know if you've got panties on under these tight as fuck skinny jeans. I wanna know if I took them off if your pussy would be wet and waiting? Is it bare or trimmed? My vote is on bare, with you being a swimmer and all."

My cheeks glow. I wasn't expecting that to come out of his mouth. My warm, flushed chest rises and falls as my breathing picks up to another level. With the change, I grow acutely aware of every single inch of him that's touching me. My voice turns a bit breathily unintentionally, "Jesus, is that the only thing ever on your mind?"

He shrugs unabashed. "When it comes to you, it is. I know what I want."

I clear my throat, working on getting my wits about me. It'd be too easy to lay down and let him ravage me, but I can't let that happen. He can't distract me from the main reason why I'm here. "I-I'm here for my sister." Am I reminding him or me at this point? Who knows, but clearly, I need to hear it as well.

He clicks his tongue. "Right. You still haven't given me what I wanted for it, Gem."

"I offered to pay you! I even let you kiss me!" I reply in outrage. This man has some brass balls like no other.

He chuckles, the move vibrating me through his chest. I should probably dislike it, but it warms my belly. Even if it does seem to sound more sinister than sweet. His hand goes to the back of my neck, pulling me in closer to him. His lips merely a hair away from mine, graze my mouth as he lowly grumbles, "You wanted that kiss. Your mouth practically begged for it." I taste the alcohol on his breath, the sensation wanting me to experience it on his tongue as well.

I let out a pathetic whimper. I turn to putty around this jerk of a man, and he can see right through me. "Please," I end up whispering, no longer able to fight the tension between us, and then his lips crash against mine. *What am I doing? Was I begging for information or another kiss?* I couldn't even say. And why don't I care about the possible repercussions? It's like I've come to Texas and thrown my trepidations with this man and his club right out the window.

My hands go to his shoulders, quickly rubbing over his solid muscles to tangle my fingers together behind his neck. The hand he's previously clamped down tightly on my hip releases enough to snake around my middle. His palm splays open across my stomach, covering a decent portion, and with it, a zap of sensation works its way from his touch straight to my core. His fingers are large enough to graze the underside of my breast, making me squirm. He does it several times, shifting his finger back and forth, eliciting goosebumps over my flesh. I wish he was touching my skin and not my thin blouse. He has me silently wishing we had no clothes between us at all.

His blissful assault on my mouth makes me grow bold, and I'm soon moving around to straddle my legs on either side of his hips. He pulls me to him with each caress of our tongues, the new position allowing me to mold my body to his. He's solid in all the places I'm soft, and I find myself wanting to rub over him like a cat in heat. My ample chest presses firmly against his hard pecs, the sensation of my nipples hardening through the lacy bra has me wanting to pant with desire. Our kiss morphs to a full-on make-out session, his mouth leaving mine to nip and kiss over my throat. His grip pulls me to him, and my core rubs against his long hardness shamelessly. If the amount I shift my hips is anything to go on, this man's cock is huge. He could do some serious damage in the best sort of way.

He starts to suck where my neck meets my shoulder, and a moan escapes me. His hips jolt at the sound, the stiffness coming in direct contact with my clit. My head falls forward as I bite back another throaty, wanton moan. I'm going to orgasm from dry humping him alone. This may end up being the best day I've had all month.

"Let's go to my room," he suggests on a husky rasp. "I'd make you feel good right here, but you strike me as a woman who enjoys her privacy more than being on show. I don't want you holding back on me. I want to hear you scream my name as I rip your pussy wide open with my cock and relish in your moans of pleasure."

His words clear away a bit of the haze his kiss had expertly woven around me. Picking my head up, my heavy lids part, and I shake my head. "I can't…"

He snorts, not believing it for an instant. He does whatever he wants, so why should I be any different in his eyes? "You can do whatever the fuck you want. I won't let anyone stop ya."

I shake my head, this time with more emphasis. "No. I mean, I came here to find out about my sister. I was hoping you'd be more forthcoming with Madison's whereabouts this time around. I didn't come here for this."

He releases a dejected grunt, and my hands go to his cheeks. What is it about this guy that makes me want to touch him? When did I gain so much courage as to not be intimidated by someone like him? He's the type of man who wrecks women, and that alone doesn't seem to sway me away when it should. "Well, that's a shame, Gem."

I know he's not a good guy. The team thoroughly researched the Royal Bastards after we'd left last time. They didn't find much, but what they did discover wasn't anything to write home about. They're an outlaw one percenter motorcycle club who've been persons of interest in several cases that include trafficking, drugs, and murder. Those were the only things on record we could dig into. That's not including the things that go under the radar. Those articles weren't all aimed at Texas either. I guess this motorcycle club is pretty nasty all over the states. Their patch comes with a hefty price. The men in this club join and only leave in a body bag, and here I am, making out with one of the presidents. To wear the rank he does, he has to be one of the worst around, yet I've got some sort of blinders on where Ripper's concerned.

If my father knew, he'd be puking his guts up like it were election day. My mother would be outraged, though she'd live vicariously through my stories. I love her beyond measure, but my mother's a hypocrite. Madison, on the other hand, would more than likely jump in to join the party and ask if drugs were available as well. I love my sister, but sometimes I wonder how on earth she's related to us. We're far too conservative, in *her* opinion. I wonder how straitlaced she'd believe I was if she could see me out here grinding and panting on a Royal Bastard.

"You know I'm not here to cause her any harm, or your club." I meet his hazel irises, attempting to put him at ease with anything holding him back. "I only want to bring her home. J-just tell me…is she alive and okay? That's the most important thing to me at this point."

He huffs, offended at my insinuation that anyone here would possibly harm her. "Of course, she's alive." He shakes his head, and while I may have upset him, I'm glad I asked.

I release a tense breath, saying, "Thank God. We may not be super close, but I love my younger sister. I feel like a piece of me has been missing, not knowing where she is and if she's okay."

"Gem, you ever think that maybe she just isn't cut out for the senator's lifestyle? And how is it you take on so much damn responsibility? That's your parents' burden."

I nod, my back muscles less tense than a moment ago. "I understand why you say that. I really do." I go to stand and put some much-needed space between us. His hands fly to my hips, not letting me go. "I should sit over there." I gesture to the next chair. What I should do and what he wants seem to be two completely different things, however.

"Now, don't go over there 'cause I'm being real with ya. I want you here. You don't have to straddle me if you're uncomfortable, but I like you in this spot, this close. You make a good lap warmer." He attempts to make the situation lighter, and I could kiss him for trying to set my mind at ease. Madison's right. I'm uptight, even though I never realized it in the past.

He winks, and my cheeks burn again. I'm not a virgin by any means, but his attention makes me feel like one. This isn't prom, and I'm not on my first date, damn it. I'm a grown woman, and he's just…so much man, it's a lot to take in. "Okay, I can handle that," I relent. *But can I really?* I'm not so sure I could stave off his advances if he initiates another kiss. I shift, moving my leg over, so I'm no longer straddling him but sitting with my side to him.

"See, not so bad." He offers me a smug grin, eyes twinkling.

I huff out a laugh, placing my hands in my lap, not really sure what to do with them anymore. "Says the biker wanting to take me to his bedroom."

His grin expands. "I won't deny that; not ever, babe. Now, your sister was okay the last time I saw her."

My hopes skyrocket at his words. Especially since he's giving me information without any of my father's money in hand. He could've held off and waited until he was paid to say as much. "And when exactly was that?" I press on, praying he won't stop there.

He looks away, staring off into the trees for a beat before admitting, "This week."

I gasp, not expecting it to have been so soon. I was beginning to believe she was on her way to another location entirely. I was hoping one of the guys here would have a way to get in touch with her at the very least. To hear that she could still be in the same area as we are, fills my chest with excitement. I haven't felt this light since she was home and safe. "This week?" I repeat, wanting to hear it again.

He grunts. "Yep. I'm telling you, Gem, you shouldn't worry about her like you do. She doesn't deserve it."

My brow wrinkles. "Of course, she does; she's my sister."

He cracks his neck and rumbles. "Not how I meant that to come out. She was partying and getting down with the brothers. I don't think it's fair for you to be worrying your pretty little head over someone who's been having that much of a good time is all."

I bite the inside of my cheek. It hurts to hear she wasn't worried about upsetting her family, but I'm not surprised. My sister has always been selfish. "I understand, but it's something I can't help. I've always looked for her, so it's in me to worry about her. Madison doesn't always make the best decisions, and I'd hate for something bad to happen to her."

"I got you, babe. Now, tell me what your dad has to offer for her." I go to shift off his lap again, and he holds firm. He grows serious, staring me down. "Not being a dick or anything. You said he'd pay, and I'm a businessman."

I nod, still not happy that he's willing to blackmail my father for my sister. "He will. I wasn't lying."

"Didn't think you were, or I wouldn't have said shit until I spoke to Maddy about it. We may seem to be a bunch of scoundrels, but we do have a sense of loyalty. Where your sister is concerned, she's an adult, so it's not really my place to give her up if she doesn't want that. However, I'm a businessman and money talks. If your pops wants to pay, then who are we to not point him in the right direction—for a friend, that is." He shrugs with the last part, staring me down. While he says he's doing this for money, something tells me it's not that at all, that maybe—just maybe—it's because of me.

"What kind of businessman?" I venture, wanting to dig a little deeper into the man himself. I shouldn't care, but something propels me to want to know anything about him I can. Ripper is a bad boy enigma where I'm concerned, and it's got my mind going wild for any information I can get on him.

"Not the good kind, Gem," he presses a kiss to my nose. It's sweet, and it has my heart pitter-pattering in response. "Now, make the call to your daddy, and let's get this deal underway."

Chapter 8

> If you don't like where you are,
> move. You are not a tree.
> -Tattify

Ripper

My cock is still aching from having Alice rub all over it yesterday during our little impromptu visit. She'd gotten me so fucking worked up, I thought the stiff bastard was never going down again. I'd cut our chat short, knowing that if I didn't, I'd end up taking her to my spot and fuck her raw. I wasn't about to let my cock jeopardize a payday for the club, and Lord knows it would've had she remained on my lap for much longer. The things I sacrifice for this club. I swear, my brothers better be fucking grateful.

"What's the deal, brother?" Whiskey grumbles as I lean back into my spiffy new office chair. With as much time as I spend in this damn room, I had the prospect run to Sam's club and get me this fancy padded shit. Now my ass is so comfortable here, I could take a nap.

"Alice texted me." I shrug it off like it doesn't mean anything, although it's driving me a bit crazy, to be honest.

"Why's this have you fucked in the head?"

I shoot a scowl at the old bastard. "You're fucked in the head."

He snorts, ignoring me.

Eventually, I continue with, "Her father doesn't want her returning to the club. He's gonna fly down to do the exchange for Maddy. Blow's gonna take her to the swap since she'll go with him and not ask any questions. I don't like it that this motherfucker thinks he can call the shots while he's up north doin' fuck all. A real man would contact me and hash this shit out. Clearly, this fucker didn't get that memo."

"And this has you questioning things, why? Who gives a fuck, minus we get paid."

I shrug, stubbornly admitting, "I was expecting Alice to be around until that all went down. She said now her security is tighter than usual, stuck up her ass and all. Her father's afraid she'll mess up the deal somehow before it has a chance to happen. He needs to get it through his thick skull that Alice is the only reason this shit is happening in the first place. Bougie motherfucker thinks I'm bowing cause he's a politician. Those ass sniffers can blow each other, as far as I'm concerned."

"He's a real piece of work."

I nod. "And she doesn't see it. He's got his family blinded, all in the disguise of protection. The fucker's a crook. Takes one to know one, ya know?"

"Hm, those types usually are. Can't say I'm all that surprised. Still don't understand what's eating you though. We're getting paid and didn't have to do shit. It sounds like a win to me. Is this the only thing weighing on you?"

"Oh, no doubt."

"You wanted to fuck her, and it actually didn't happen," he comments after a beat, bursting into a belly laugh. The dick is one of the only bastards who can get a read on me.

"Fuck off, you old bastard," I gripe while he continues to chuckle at my expense.

"So, let me get this straight. You're intrigued by this senator's daughter, and they've caged her up like a little birdy. Since when have you ever let someone stand in the way of what you want? She can't come to you…but there's not a fuckin' thing stoppin' your stubborn ass from going to her."

After a beat, his words sink in, and I crack a grin. "You smart, wrinkly, bastard."

He shoots me the bird, and I pull Alice's name up on my phone.

How bored are you? I ask her.

This sounds like a loaded question. She responds and I find myself smiling like a jackass.

I could visit. I throw the suggestion out, hoping she'll send an invitation.

My security wouldn't let you in the door.

A snort of disbelief escapes. She has no idea of what I'm capable of. **They couldn't stop me no matter how hard they tried.**

I don't want them to end up hurt. Despite the tense meetings we've had, they're good guys.

"I hope she's sending you titty pics with the size of the smile you've got on," Whiskey complains, but I ignore him. He's just bent out of shape 'cause he hasn't gotten laid in a while.

I remain focused on Alice. **I can make it so they never know I'm there.**

How? She immediately asks.

Invite me over and find out.

If you won't hurt anyone, then come see me.

Send me the address and room number. I'll swing by tonight. "I need a sweetbutt," I say and get to my feet.

"Ah, you came up with a plan already?"

I nod to Whiskey. "Of course, I'll be back."

I head for the bar. It figures, the one time I'm searching out some easy pussy, it's nowhere to be found. Usually any of the girls around here are trying to stroke on my dick. Manic is sitting on his ass watching a basketball game on the oversized TV in the small rec room we have. It's for the brothers only, so the room is usually empty. I've learned over the years that men are where drugs, alcohol, or pussy is, if it's available.

"Hey, Prospect?"

He twists around, and when he sees it's me hollering for him, he jumps to his feet. He reminds me of Plague. It's no wonder they're close. "Prez? What can I do for you?"

"You seen any gash around?"

He nods. "Yeah. Blow took Maddy in his room. Powerhouse left with Delilah to the strip club for work, and Cindy was taking a nap on the back porch. You want me to get one of the girls for you?"

"Bet. Nah, finish your game. I can get Cindy on my own…need to discuss some shit with her anyhow."

He nods, and plops back in his spot. Lazy fucker's probably hungover.

We have a hammock on the back porch that the bitches are always in. I should've guessed one of them would be there now. I find her softly snoring, her red hair twisted up in a top knot. She's got on some spandex shorts and a T-shirt. The shirt's cut up, falling off one shoulder and tied up to show off her flat tummy. "Cindy!" I boom out, startling her. My mouth lifts as I chuckle at her expression. She jumps awake instantly, eyes wide in panic.

Her hand flies to her chest. "Prez! You about gave me a heart attack!" she says breathily, and I chuckle harder.

"Sorry 'bout that," I offer disingenuously.

She catches her breath, moving to sit up. I hold the hammock so she can get her feet to the ground and not send herself sprawling to the deck. I may poke fun at spooking her, but I don't want her to physically hurt herself on my account. "Are you looking to get sucked off?" She eventually asks, licking her lips. She's got a real pout on her; the brothers shell out for her injections. They love 'em, but the fat lips aren't really my thing, even when it comes to a blow job.

"Nah, darlin,' I've come to ask for your help."

She beams wide, standing to her full height. She's a tiny spitfire, I'd guess about five foot six or so. "Anything, Prez, just name it."

"That's a good girl." I nod approvingly, and she glows with my praise. "Did you see those three guys come in here yesterday with the woman?"

"It was kind of hard to miss with all the tension. I stayed back in the hall, figured a fight would go down and someone would get hurt. Them, of course," she reassures.

"Of course. Anyhow, I need to get into a hotel room, and at least one of those guys will need distracting, could be more than one though. Think you could handle that job for me?"

"Point me in their direction, and I'll make sure they never see you."

"You make that happen, and I'll let the brothers know we can count on you, Cindy."

She lights up again at my words. It's a sweetbutt's dream to have favor with the brothers. Not that anything would ever come of it, but what she doesn't know won't hurt. "It's an honor, Prez, really." She nearly vibrates with excitement. I'm asking her to suck or fuck a random man and she's thanking me for it. How ironic, but I won't argue, that's for damn sure.

"All right, be ready at eleven tonight. Wear something real sexy—the shorter, the better. We'll ride over when most of the hotel has turned in and put the plan in action."

Until then, I wait...and remind myself that nothing good ever comes easy, and I'm okay with that. I'm used to working for what I want, and right now, that's Alice Compton—naked, beneath me.

Cindy holds on to me tightly as we ride through the mild night to Alice's hotel. There's nothing like riding at night or early morning in Texas. It gives you an exhilarating rush that you feel all over. It's hard to explain, but it's addictive. There's something in the air that's relaxing and makes the pride swell in your chest for the Lonestar state. I couldn't imagine ever living somewhere else. This place has always been home and will continue to be until I take my last breath.

I pull into the hotel's parking lot and park on the opposite side of where her room should be located, in the pitch black. I don't want any of her suits popping their head in the window at the sound of my pipes and see us coming. I stick to the shadows, as I do often. They say scary things wait for you in the shadows, but in my case, I am the motherfucking monster.

"Oh, spooky, Prez, hm?" Cindy hums, an underlying Jersey accent making its presence known. I doubt any of the brothers have caught it before, but it's my job to notice the little things. Sometimes the most important things are the ones people believe aren't significant.

"You better watch that tone darlin', or people will catch on that you're not a true Southerner." I take in the worried gaze she casts me as the streetlamp picks up our presence. "Your secret's safe with me, but I'm bettin' you're escaping something out there."

"Thanks, Prez," she whispers, her gaze falling to the sidewalk. She doesn't speak on it any further, but she's like an open book. She's got her own ghosts, but I'm not trying to dig into those right now.

"Shake it off, honey. You've got a job to do, and I need your head in the game."

Cindy flashes a smile. It's more for her sake than mine, though; I don't need a lift. She retorts, "You got it."

"If we're quiet, the night clerk won't hear us. She's usually in the back watching videos on her phone from what Alice has told me."

"She sneak out of here a lot?"

"No, she swims." I don't know why I go as far as sharing that detail about Alice. Lord knows it's not the sweetbutt's business, by any means. Maybe I'm trying to be nice after calling her out a moment ago. Whatever the case, no one should get used to it. I'm a bastard through and through—always have been, always will be. "We'll ride the elevator up to the third floor. You'll go down the hall first, and I'll wait five minutes to give you a chance to distract her security. Now, remember, I need you to get him or them to have their back to me so I can get by and to the room."

"You think this Alice woman is something special, huh?"

"Don't go reaching, Cindy; this is business. You want to earn the brothers' favor, right?"

She nods adamantly as the electric doors swish apart. I grab her bicep and yank her with me as we quickly duck inside and past the check-in desk. The elevators are off to the side with a wall as a barrier, so I tug her to the door before peeking my head around the corner to check the front. The clerk never looks to see who came in, so we're in the clear.

"We're good. Now the second part of the plan," I say and hit the *up* button on the pair of elevators. The one on the right chimes immediately, having been sitting on the ground floor and lets us inside. I press the illuminated three and we ride up the few levels until the door automatically opens again. "Showtime, darlin'," I hiss and give the gash a shove in the appropriate direction.

She disappears around the corner, and I hold my breath to listen. I can hear voices, though they're not loud enough for me to make out the words. I tug my cell out of my breast pocket in my cut and type out a text to Alice.

Count to eighty and open the door to your room a crack.

Why? She questions and I huff to myself.

Just do it, got a surprise for you.

She responds with a smile emoji, and I tuck my phone away. I start walking to the end of the hall, counting to myself. I make it there by number twenty-six and I listen for Cindy and the security team. I hear her make a gagging sound and chance peeking around the corner. She's got him in the far corner. Looks like she's on her knees with him hiding her. His back's to me just as I'd told her to do. I slowly walk toward Alice's room, not wanting to alert them to my presence. As soon as the right door cracks open, I push into it, ducking inside. I'm met with her mouth hanging open, gaping at me.

"You're here!" she whispers. "Oh, my God. I didn't think you'd actually come!"

I grin. "Told ya, babe."

Her finger flies to her lips, telling me not to speak. She holds out a finger, instructing me to wait a minute, and she heads into the bathroom. A beat later and the shower's turned on full blast, the sound of water filling the room. She comes out again, still with that same finger up. I watch as she takes off her fancy round diamond earrings, places them on the dresser next to the TV, which she turns up as well and then steps back to me. Her hand finds mine, then she's tugging me into the bathroom with her, closing the door behind us.

"They can hear everything. I have to be careful," Alice says, eyes wide as the room already begins to fill with steam.

"The walls are thin, Gem, but they can't hear us in here with the water goin' and the door shut."

"It's not that; there's listening devices, in case I'm in trouble. This is the only way we can have some privacy...well, as long as we don't speak too loudly or they'll pick up on that too."

"Shit, baby." My brow shoots up in surprise. Listening devices, hm? What a bunch of dicks to obtain so much control over her. No wonder she was bored. She literally can't have anything to herself—no conversations, even on the phone. That's fucked up. It pisses me off, but I keep those thoughts to myself. I'm here to take her mind off those things and bring a little fun into her night.

I flash her a naughty grin. "Hope you can be quiet then."

She giggles. I love the sound and lean in, taking her lips with mine. She's in an oversized button-down shirt, the shiny baby pink, satiny pajama kind. I didn't go to this much trouble to see her in clothes, so I grab the front of it and rip it apart down the middle. The black buttons go flying in every direction, and the beautiful woman before me gasps in shock. I push the short matching shorts off her hips to discover she's not wearing anything underneath those pajamas.

A growl escapes as my rough palms finally come in contact with the tender flesh of her plump, heavy breasts. Her nipples tickle the middle of my palms, and I can no longer hold myself back. Breaking contact with her mouth, I dip my head, drawing the sweet bud between my lips. My teeth graze her soft, creamy skin as I suck and knead the delicate flesh. I want to leave hickeys on her tits that're bigger than her fucking nipples. I want them to look like they're double in size. For some reason that thought makes me go insane for her. Everything about this gorgeous woman before me, has me wanting to mark her up with my mouth and my cum.

"Cold or hot?" I grate out between my tongue toying with the stiff peaks.

She hums with pleasure. Her hands grip my short-styled hair tightly, occasionally tugging on the hazelnut locks. She's going to drive me mad; the sensation has thoughts of eating her pussy spiraling through me. She'd be pulling my hair then, that's for sure, as I'd ravage the fuck outta her sweet cunt. I'd have the sexy bitch ride my tongue until she orgasmed so many times it made her ass pass the fuck out.

"Tell me what you want, or I'll decide for you," I threaten.

"W-what? I can't think while you do that." Her palm lands on my chin, pulling my head upwards. I meet her gaze, her titty leaving my mouth with a pop. I wasn't ready to give it back to her.

"The shower, Gem. You like your water hot or cold?"

"Oh," she puffs out, her cheeks and chest flushed with desire. Her irises are dilated, tattling that she wants me to continue, even if she were to tell me no. The body doesn't lie, and hers is giving me green lights everywhere. "Hot or even warm is good, I'm not picky."

My hand shoots into the spray, making sure it's not icy cold. I carefully pull my cut off, folding it and placing it on the high-end marble countertop. I rip my T-shirt over my head, tossing it at the mirror. Next, I move to toe off my boots, and then shove my jeans down my hips. I'm moving too fast and my hands get caught in the material as I try to be rid of it all. Her mouth parts, her chest rising and falling quickly as she watches my unsexy show of discarding my clothes.

Gazing at her like this, finally naked before me, has me taking stock in our differences. We're opposites. For starters, the woman doesn't have a tattoo or piercing in sight. I, on the other hand, am covered in ink and have a variety of piercings. Hell, even my cock is pierced. I've got one on the top and one on the bottom. I like covering all my bases when it comes to pounding a pussy the right way. I hope hers is ready for me, I'm about to change her outlook on sex forever.

Chapter 9

> What matters most is how well
> you walk through the fire.
> - Charles Bukowski

Alice

"I-is that really a piercing down there?" I can't help but ask. *I swear if his length gets any bigger than he is now, he may not fit. Am I really doing this right now?* I haven't had a moment to stop and think, one second he was texting, and the next he was ripping my clothes off. I've never had this kind of explosive chemistry with someone before, and it's overwhelming. I barely know this man, yet it's been a whirlwind of sexual attraction and tension building up between us.

He flashes an arrogant grin. "Yeah, my cock's pierced. Up top and down below."

Sweet Jesus. And his nipples are pierced as well. He's a canvas of art and metal, everything I'm not and everything I've never had before. I've never wanted someone so badly either. I can feel the moisture gathering between my legs, pooling like I'm a sex starved maniac. It's rather embarrassing, to be frank. I'm insanely turned on, and there's no way I can hide it if he touches me.

"You're huge," I breathe.

He nods, taking a step closer. He's a hair's width away from touching me, his cock on my belly. "I'm called Ripper for a reason, Gem. I thought you knew as much."

I shake my head. I thought I had a clue, but I had absolutely no idea. Sure, grinding on him yesterday let me feel him through his pants, but it was nothing in comparison to seeing him in his full glory. He must make men wither away in shame when he uses a public restroom.

"The piercings will help soothe the ache. You just let me fuck you like I know how you need it, and you'll survive."

A squeak escapes me. It was meant to be a whimper, but it didn't quite make it that far. I'm in so far over my head with this man, yet I can't help it. No matter how much I try to fight the pull between us, it just never stops. His finger goes to my chin, holding it in place as he leans in. He tenderly brushes his mouth against mine—once, twice, three times—before winking. He doesn't even have to ask. I'm putty in this man's hands, willing to let him do whatever he wants. Yet, he waits for my consent, and I offer it with a tilt of my head. Any more of his delicious torture and I'll be begging for his touch.

It's the breaking point for him, and in my next breath, he's hauled me up in his arms. It takes everything in me to keep quiet. He lifts me as if I'm nothing, my legs wrapping around his strong hips like they're used to doing this very thing with him. With one hand holding me firmly to him, he uses the other on the shower wall to step inside. Thankfully, this place has a separate garden tub, or we may've fallen and thrown out our backs. Though, with Ripper, I doubt he ever allows something so trivial to get in his way of fucking.

The warm spray hits me from the side as I'm pressed up against the far wall. Ripper's mouth goes to my throat, nipping and sucking, hitting all the ultra-sensitive places I never realized I had. He makes me feel like a fish out of water, and I've had sex several times over the years, yet it's all new with him. "Oh, God," I moan.

His chest vibrates with a chuckle. "I'm barely kissing you, baby. Wait until I start fuckin' you. And say my name, yeah?"

"Ripper," I gasp the next time he bites down, and I'm rewarded with a pleased groan from him. The water makes everything slippery, but he holds me to him like a vice, his cock lining up right with my core. There's nothing between us, just warm water and body heat. "Condom," I say breathlessly as he rubs his massive cock against my clit.

"I'm clean."

"We have to use a condom," I say, and he grumbles.

"I'd never hurt you like that."

"I-I believe you," I pant as his cock presses against me and serious zings of sensations spiral through me. "I'm not on birth control. I ran out and haven't been here long enough to have it transferred."

"Mm, gotcha. While you'd look sexy as fuck with a belly made round by me, I'm not so sure you'd feel the same way." He chuckles and I offer him an amused smile. Pregnancy is nowhere near the front of my mind, especially not in a situation like this. "I have one in my wallet, give me a sec." He hops out of the water, returning moments later with a Magnum. The square looks super-sized and when I flick my gaze down, I see he's grown bigger than before.

"Oh my God," I mutter, not realizing I said the words aloud. "Huge."

He follows my gaze, and if I didn't know any better, I'd swear the fearless biker blushes. "I know I'm not average...I know how to use it, though."

A laugh bubbles free. "Oh, there's nothing about you that's average; that, I can assure you."

He smirks. "I'll take that as a compliment, then."

"Good, you should."

At my words, he gains his confidence right back and rolls on the condom. He saunters over to me, allowing me a moment to appreciate his fantastic form. In the next breath, he has me lifted and wrapped around his robust physique just as before. His right-hand trails down my figure. He lightly pinches my nipple before continuing on. He softly squeezes my hip bone, then dives between my thighs. His fingers smooth through my wetness, a sigh of delight leaving him when he finds out how truly turned on I am. He has my pussy so creamy, he could thrust all the way inside me with that massive cock of his if he desired it. Rather than rip me apart right away, he inserts one finger, pumping the digit a few times before slipping another inside.

"Yes," I hiss with delight, wanting everything he'll give me. "More," I demand, and he obliges. With a third finger, he pushes in deep, and I moan. His mouth smothers mine, stealing the sound with his tongue. My hips follow his hand, wanting him to punish my pussy. It's been far too long since I've been touched, and he's making all the right moves.

"Gotta get you ready," he rasps, breaking the kiss.

"I-I am."

"You sure about that, Gem? I don't want to hurt you too badly. My cock was created to torment little pussies."

"Please," I beg, wishing I could claw his flesh with nails I don't have. "I want you so bad."

"So bad?" he taunts. The bastard's used to begging from women, that I don't doubt for a second.

"Give me your cock, Ripper. Hurt my pussy."

"Just remember, you asked for it. Tomorrow when you can't pee or walk, remember this moment."

I nearly snarl in frustration. The man has me vibrating with need. He's a damn tease. His hands lock onto my hips and then he's filling me. In one punishing thrust, he splits my pussy open to make room for his girth. I'll never be the same; I know this already. There's not another man out there that'll satisfy me like he can. "Oh!" I cry, and his hand covers my mouth. His lips nip at my ear lobe as he tucks his face in next to mine.

"Shh, not too loud, remember? Though I don't mind beating some ass after I fuck this tight pussy of yours. Just say the word, baby, and no one will be able to keep you from me."

How can his violent words turn me on so much? They do, though. His brash assholeness is an aphrodisiac on my mind. He strums my body violently with his cock while whispering threats to anyone who dares get in his way when it comes to me. It draws me in, more and more, making me imagine him actually doing it. I'm a nonviolent person. I like peace and compassion, but his intense passion is quickly snuffing it all out. The way he touches me, the way he is…it's addicting.

"You'd hurt them for me?" I breathe the question, panting between the words. He has my pussy so needy, I keep clamping down on his long shaft each time he hits me deep.

His eyes flair, his teeth gritting together as he watches me writhe in pleasure. "Fuck, yes," he proclaims and slams home. It's too much, too deep, and I cry out. He'd dropped his hand away from my mouth and I went and practically told on myself. No one has heard him come in my room, though, so my guards will think I'm in the shower pleasuring myself. It'll be hard for them to believe, as it hasn't happened in the past where they could overhear, but there's a first time for everything.

"You like that? Feeling me fuck you hard, knowing I'm tearing that sweet little pussy open for my cock?"

"God, yes!" I shamelessly relent. He's good, far too good, that there's no way I'll even attempt to deny it. His strong body holds me in place as I rub my hands over each dip and swell of hardened muscle. He's more man than I've had my hands on before. He puts those straitlaced proper guys to shame with his filthy mouth and monstrous cock.

"I'm close," I choke out, growing more desperate with each thrust.

He takes my words to heart, his grip tightening as he bares down and slams into me. He bends his knees and drives his cock upwards in short, ruthless thrusts. His pelvis hits my clit repeatedly, the sensations so overwhelming that tears spring to my eyes. I feel like I have a hurricane brewing inside, and it keeps swirling bigger as my orgasm nears. This man doesn't fuck, *he consumes,* taking ownership to any pussy he touches. No wonder why my sister didn't want to come home if she's being fucked like this. It'd be hard for me to think straight enough to make it back myself.

"You're so fucking sexy—and this body, babe. You're the type of bitch that drives a brother insane with lust. I've thought of nothing else but dipping inside this pussy from the moment I laid eyes on ya."

I should be appalled, completely offended that he just referred to me in that sense. I'm not. If anything, his words throw me into a tailspin. I feel desired, ridiculously beautiful and sensual in his gaze, and that's a heady feeling for a woman to experience. It's a sense of power at its finest to know a man wants you that badly. Especially someone like Ripper who's fucked his share of women—all beautiful in their own sense, no doubt.

"Oh, yes!" I cry, grinding my soaked pussy against him as my peak nears. The water's ice cold, but I don't pay any attention to it. He has me overheated, warmed by his big body pressed against mine. "Yes!" I repeat and he growls ferociously, his teeth sinking into the top of my breast. My eyelids flutter closed, my head falling backward. It slams against the tile, but the shock of pain does nothing. I'm riding too high on my tumultuous orgasm to pay attention to anything other than myself and the man ramming my pussy.

"I'm going to come. Fuck, I wish I could come inside this pussy," he groans against my breast and bites the opposite globe. His cum floods the condom, his shaft throbbing with each blistering jet of seed. My pussy tenses and releases with each pulse, the feeling sends delightful aftershocks through my body, making me crave more.

It's a good thing he's holding me up, because I'd be Jell-O on the floor of the shower right now. "Wow…just wow," I hum, tucking my face into his neck. The spray hasn't completely chased away his scent of leather and sage. It makes me want to taste his flesh and continue the exploration by discovering every inch of this man.

"I'm not done, Gem."

"Huh?" I ask, suddenly feeling a bit sleepy now that I've been sated.

Ripper wraps his arms around my back, holding my frame to his tightly. I feel warm and safe and overall completely satisfied. I'm content after a day of thinking about him, and believing I was never going to see him again.

"Cover my earrings with a towel," I whisper into his ear, remembering that the guys can hear us as Ripper carries me to my plush king hotel bed. He turns down the ivory comforter and drops me right in the middle. I stay exactly where he sets me, naked and bared for his eyes. He grabs my diamond earrings that cost my father a ridiculous amount, wrapping them securely in a thick bath towel the size of a small blanket. He takes the towel back to the bathroom, leaving it behind on the counter and shuts the door. "What are you doing?" I inquire, thinking that maybe he plans to sleep in my bed with me. As much as I'd enjoy it, it's too risky, my security detail would figure out he's here, and they'd alert my father to it. That's the last thing I need when I'm so close to having my sister back.

He flashes me a devious grin, sliding between my thighs from the foot of the bed. He tosses my feet over each shoulder. "We're gonna play a game."

"Hm?" I smile in return, curious as to what he's got in mind. I have a feeling it has to do with us being naked, and I like that idea already, although my pussy is throbbing from his size, begging me for a reprieve. This may never happen to me again, so there's no way I'm going to give in to the soreness and not take full advantage of these moments with Ripper.

"We're gonna call it, *how quiet can Gem be?*"

Releasing an amused laugh, my brow rises. "Is that so? And who says I'll be the one needing to be quiet?" I challenge. His head dips between my thighs and my hands fly to cover my mouth. His tongue lavishes my pussy in long strokes and I know I've already lost this game in the best sort of way.

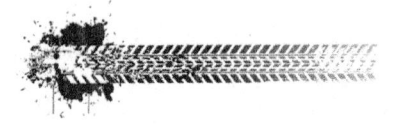

Over the next week, each evening is close to the same. Ripper sneaks into my room somehow, and brings me hours of pleasure, then he skirts by my security detail in the early hours of morning to go back to his club. Rather than reach my fill of him, I find myself growing desperate by the hour to have more of him. Each night his promises grow bolder, his remarks filthier and it turns me into a writhing, panting, hot mess for him. My pussy is absolutely wrecked. I've been soaking in hot baths with Epsom salts each morning, and yet I still beg him to brutalize my core. The pain is encased in pleasure and a sick satisfaction knowing an outlaw is hooked on having me whenever he possibly can.

My father will be here soon, and thoughts of leaving are bombarding me, putting me on edge. To be on edge is dangerous, because you stop caring as much. In my case, I've quit attempting to mask my moans at night. I've gotten so loud during my multiple orgasms that the team won't look me in the eye the next morning. I should be embarrassed, but I'm not. Truth be told, I don't care in the slightest and find the whole thing funny. What can they do? Demand me to stop pleasuring myself, or tell my father I'm up all night, enraptured in bliss? They don't know it's Ripper in my room making me feel these things, so they have nothing to go on, and proper etiquette insists they act like it never happened in the first place.

As our nights grow longer together, the days until I leave grow shorter. That knowledge has one thought popping out to me: I don't want to go home. I'm not ready. For once in my life, I understand how my younger sister must feel when faced with turning back to a life without any passion in it. I love my parents and I'm proud of my father for what he's done for the country and our family, but I want to run away now too. I want to have my own life that isn't in the campaign spotlight—one where I can make questionable decisions and relish in the feelings afterward.

Ripper has told me he wants more time with me, but is that when we're naked, or in general? Whatever it is, I need to figure out a way to make it happen. I need to change my life.

Chapter 10

*The day I changed was the day I
quit trying to fit into a world that
never really fit me.*
- JM Storm

Ripper

"What made you like this?" Alice questions one night after I'd spent a good hour tasting her sweet pussy. She'd writhed and begged and cried my name as I'd made her come three times. It was pure bliss to my ears and my taste buds.

"Excuse me? What's that supposed to mean?" We've been talking some after we fuck, getting more acquainted with each other. I've never been much of a cuddler, but with

Alice, I can't seem to get enough. I want to be near her constantly.

"It doesn't mean anything. I'm only attempting to discover more about you and what influenced your decisions to become the president of a motorcycle club." She says it all formal in her uppity dialog I've grown fond of listening to. She's not snobby or anything. She's never once looked down her nose on my club, and it has me questioning how she could've turned out so different from her parents.

I offer up a smirk. "Oh, I get it. You think something happened in my life for me to be this way? Women are always so quick to judge," I throw out, putting my guard up. It's dangerous getting close to a woman and spending this much time with her when you know she's going to leave and never spare a glance backward. It's askin' for a broken heart, and black hearts make bikers bitter. I'm already a fucking bastard to everyone, I don't need anything more spurring me on to be any worse.

"Look, I only asked because something must've propelled you to become so hardened on the outside."

I snort. This woman has nerve to bring up my transgressions when her own family can't seem to keep their shit together. "You believe that something has to happen to a person for them to turn out the way they do...but have you ever considered that some people are born this way? That I *was born this way?"

"And what way is that, exactly?"

"Bad, Gem. I'm a deplorable man, and to answer your question, there's nothing. I wasn't traumatized or any other horrendous scenario you wanna conjure up to possibly justify my actions. I was born rotten. I'm corrupt and break the law because I want to, because I enjoy doing so. Ain't no motherfucker lead me down this path but myself."

I watch her throat work as she swallows tightly. She wasn't expecting this conversation to turn in this direction, but she should've known better than to pop off and ask someone what's wrong with them. I'm a fucking asshole biker, yet I know better than that. This woman does things to me; I won't lie on that front, but she still has that uppity rich bitch running in her blood. I can't blame her for it, as she was just trying to insinuate. She's a product of her own environment. She's learning firsthand not to believe everything her father feeds her about the outside world.

"You want me to judge you on your life?" I toss out, turning this around on her. "Should I expect you to look down on me because I am who I am, and you are who you are?"

She releases a tense breath, "Ripper..." Alice says my name on a whisper. It's like a motherfucking caress to my ears. She knows how to reel me in and keep my ass wrapped around her finger. "I'm sorry...I didn't mean to offend you. I want to know you...that's all."

Scrubbing my hand over my face, my shoulders drop, and I exhale a sigh. "Fuck, Gem. I didn't mean to bite your head off...I'm used to people looking down their noses at me. I don't ever want to be there in your gaze. You feel me?"

"You won't...I promise you. I'll never see you like that. You have nothing to prove to me. My father is his own person, as am I. I told you before, I accept you for who you are and respect it."

"I've done so much shit, Alice; if you knew the half of it, you'd run far away. Hell, you should've run the first time I laid eyes on you."

She gives me a tender smile and leans in. Her lips lightly graze mine, the sensation sending tingles through my body. "It's too late. I don't want to be away from you. I'm not running anywhere."

"That so?" I reply huskily, my thoughts twisting in another direction. My hands go to her hips, working to scoot her body closer to mine. I can't seem to get enough of this woman. My feelings keep building and that feeling is both enthralling and frightening of its own accord. I rest my leg over hers, wanting to hold her but not suffocate her either. I'm not a dumbass, even I know I can come off as overwhelming at times.

"Yep, I don't care if my father doesn't like it. I'm an adult, and if that means I stay in town a little while longer to get to know you better, then I will. I have my own money; he doesn't need to pay for my hotel. He may be the senator, but he doesn't control everything. I've been thinking about this all week, a way to get him to loosen my leash."

I lean back, the thought hitting me out of nowhere. "You're a fuckin' genius, babe."

"Oh, yeah?" She giggles. "I think I like where this is headed."

"Fuck, yeah. You just gave me an idea of how to get Baker back."

"Umm, who's Baker? Is this something I can help with?"

"Baker's our brother; he's a member of the club. I need influence from someone in government, and your father may be the key. Say, Gem, how keen is your pops on asking for favors from people?"

She shrugs. "I mean, he has before, but I'm not really sure. I don't know if he can help, but I can ask if you want me to."

"Not exactly. Do you think you could get me a meeting with him?"

"He's planning on flying down here to get Madison in two days, so I don't see why not. You can bring my sister to the private air strip instead of Blow and then you'll have a chance to speak to him. I'll double check to make sure he's really coming and not sending another security detail in his place."

I lean over, pressing a quick kiss to her lips. "You're a fuckin' gem, babe."

She smirks. "So I've been told."

If I play my cards right, having Maddy and Alice around could offer the club a payday and a favor for our brother. I've learned over the years to take whatever I can get. Shit doesn't come easy, especially when you're running an mc.

"It's time for me to go," I murmur against the smooth flesh on her throat. I press a kiss there, noting the faint markings from my earlier sucking.

"I wish I could go back to the club with you," she says longingly.

"You can, just say the word. I'll stick you on the back of my bike and put you in my bed."

"You're so romantic." She rolls her eyes.

"Mm, romance is overrated. If I'm fucking you each night, making you scream my name while you come, then fuck candlelit dinners. You feel me?"

She nods silently.

"The romantic shit isn't really my thing. If that's what you want, then you'll be disappointed. I like to be balls deep inside your pussy, making you feel good in other ways. As for putting you on the back of my bike, well, you'd be the only bitch on there that wasn't a sweetbutt for the club. If you were accustomed to the MC lifestyle, then you'd understand the depth of my words."

She turns to me, offering a sweet smile before planting her lips on mine. Her kisses tie me all up inside. They make me want to grab onto her and never let go. That's a crazy ass feeling when you're normally content living the single life. This bitch has me thinking about the future and what I'd like out of it. I once believed it was financial stability, but it appears that I want a woman along with that goal.

I hit the bathroom before leaving. I shoot off a text to Cindy, to let her know I'm coming out. She's done her job well. Alice's security team have been happily sated getting their cocks sucked each night this week and part of last week as well. Cindy's kept them so distracted that I haven't been spotted once. Surely whoever's in the room next door must hear how loud Alice is, but she hasn't said anything about it, so I'm not going to pay it any mind either. She pecks a kiss on my lips as I quietly sneak back out of her room, and fuck if she doesn't drive me mad. She's left standing there in my T-shirt and a lacey pair of panties. It's quickly becoming my favorite outfit of hers aside from not wearing any clothes at all. She blows me a kiss through the crack of the door and then I'm gone, meeting Cindy downstairs. We ride back to the club in silence. We've been this way each night, lost in our own thoughts. The brothers haven't said anything about my late-night excursions just yet, but I know it's coming. I can see it in their eyes when they watch me leave at night. They have questions, and no doubt some of them are about why I'm always carting Cindy along with me.

"Hey, Prez," Blow calls through my bedroom door. "Ma's here." I scrub my hand down my face, crawling from bed. I've been sleeping later than usual since I've been staying out all night. My body's not used to it, and it's fucking up the business schedule I normally keep. Something has to give. Alice either needs to be out of my life, or more permanently in it by coming around the clubhouse. This past week with her has felt like a vacation of sorts. I've been shucking off my responsibilities to get my dick wet. A president can't do that or the club will fall to shit, and I pledged myself to this MC and my brothers to not ever allow that to happen.

"All right," I call back with a grumble when Blow bangs on my door again. "Fucker..." I gripe, yanking on some clothes and my boots. I quickly brush my teeth, all the while thinking about the jug of black coffee I intend to drink as soon as possible. I toss a glance at my alarm clock, noticing it's two p.m. Definitely living the night life. This is Plague and Manic's MO with all their partying and fucking off, not mine.

I head for the bar. There better be some strong coffee brewed or I'm liable to throat punch whichever prospect I find first. My ma's sitting at the bar, shooting the shit with Whiskey while he shoves chocolate chip cookies into his mouth like a starved bastard. She always shows up, bringing shit she's baked for us. The guys love it.

"Hey, Ma," I greet, leaning into her hug. I place a kiss on her forehead.

"Hey, baby," she says, offering me a smile. "You all right?"

I nod, as Whiskey huffs and shakes his head.

My mom glances between us, zeroing in on me. "You wanna tell me what's going on, or do you want me to find out for myself?" she threatens.

I pour coffee into the largest cup I can find with a sigh. "I'm fine, just overslept." I bring the steaming beverage with me to take the seat next to her.

Whiskey coughs out a "Bullshit."

I shoot him a glare, before offering my mom an innocent smile. It's gotten me out of so much shit in the past. She'd go soft on me when she was trying to discipline me and I knew I was in the clear. At least, until my pops found out, then he'd be through to whip my ass for whatever reason. "Whiskey's getting you stirred up for nothing." I know better than to tell her I've been only seeing one woman.

"Mmhm," he grunts. "I'm not stirring shit up. That little senorita you've been sneaking out for at night is the one stirring you up, brother."

"Fucking narc," I complain.

Whiskey offers me a shit eating grin in response, knowing that Ma will latch onto that bit and not let it go. He shrugs, not put out in the slightest. "Her cookies are too good."

"Selling me out for sugar," I gripe, taking a sip of coffee. The warmth and strong flavor explodes over my tongue. It's the best thing in the morning aside from a wet pussy.

"Oh, baby!" She draws the word out with excitement. "My boy finally has a girlfriend?"

Don't let her fool ya. She plays the innocent lady well, but's been around this life with my pop. She knows damn well I don't do girlfriends or any of that mess. I fuck sweetbutts, as do most other MC members she's known my entire life.

"You gonna make her your ol' lady?" she continues, and I groan.

"It's not like that. We're just having fun. And before you dig your claws in, relax. I've only been fucking her for a little over a week."

Her eyes light up and I shake my head. She's like a dog with a bone. "The right woman is good for a man, Ripper, especially a president of an MC."

Whiskey grins widely behind her. If she wasn't staring straight at me, I'd flip his annoying ass off. He knew exactly what he was doing, getting her on my case.

"You're a good ol' lady, Ma. Dad would be lost without you, but I'm not him. I'm not looking to settle down just yet, especially not with her…"

"Oh?" Her brow jumps. "And what's wrong with this woman you're seeing?"

"Fucking, Mom, we're fucking." Not that the crass language dissuades her. She's used to worse from her ol' man. "And to answer your question, nothing is wrong with her. We're just different people, she doesn't even live around here."

She tsks. "Your father and I didn't live near each other either. We never let distance stop us from being happy together."

I nod because there's no way I can win this with her. She doesn't need to know the details of Alice, her wild sister, or her senator father. If I'm being a realist, her father would never allow us to be together anyhow. He'd bring down the law, no doubt, if he thought I was defiling his daughter. The club's investments can't handle that close of a look. We have multiple kilos of cocaine here for fuck's sake, and we'd be doing some serious time if we were raided. Alice's pussy is sweet and all, but I'm not putting my brothers and club through that sort of struggle.

"I'm sure you have another bitch in mind for me, Ma. Maybe one who's in the life?" I can at least try to distract her, and this has to be the way to do it.

"Oh, heavens no. The young girls in your father's club are little whores. None of them are good enough for my son."

Her reply brings a wide smile to my face. Now she's sounding like my ma when it comes to females. "Who says I want a young chick?" I ask, aiming to ruffle her feathers.

"Now, now…don't be looking at any of my friends like that." She sends me a serious glance, and I burst out laughing.

"It'll happen when it's supposed to, Ma. You don't need to worry about me."

Her hand pats my scruffy cheek. "You'll understand one day when you have a kid of your own. You'll want them to have that commitment and happiness too."

"If I have a son, I'll be lining up the club whores for him."

She rolls her eyes, not replying. She sighs and stands. "I've got to be getting back. I only stopped in to bring you boys a snack. Without me around, the phone at the garage will be ringing off the hook. Lord knows your father never answers the damn thing."

I chuckle. They've been this way for as long as I can remember. My mom likes to stop over and check in on us. I think she uses the cookies as an excuse. Whiskey sure eats up the attention, and Ma treats us like we're a bunch of kids and he enjoys the fuck out of it. If he hadn't been good friends with my father for so long, I'd be worried he has the hots for my Ma, but I know his type, and she's not it. I press a kiss to the top of her head, and she tucks in under my arm for another hug.

Whiskey pauses in his munch to walk her to her car. One of the brothers always walks her out. It's for her safety and to show her the respect she deserves. Not only as my mom but as a longtime, committed ol' lady. My father doesn't belong to the Royal Bastards, but his club has never been an enemy to us either. They're treated like friends, and as long as I'm around, they always will be.

Her words did get me thinking, though. If there was a way to keep Alice around, I'd do it. I enjoy her company, and with the security detail missing, we could have some real fun together. Alice brought up the possibility of her staying back longer, but I don't know whether it'll happen or not. I'm going to play it by ear and see if she can get free from her father's hold. With the search party he sent out for Maddy, I don't see him letting up the reigns on his other daughter that easily.

One thing's for sure, I have to be at that meeting with Senator Compton.

Chapter 11

*Breathe, darling. This is just a chapter.
It's not your whole story.*
- S.C. Lourie

Alice

I'm standing in the wind on the thick, black tarmac of the private airport when the first sounds of pipes greet my ears. My father landed thirty minutes ago, and he's already wanting to get back in the air and out of Texas. Everything to him is always about the campaign and taking the time to pick up his youngest daughter is cutting into his tedious schedule. He's brought five men along from his new security detail that I hadn't previously met to assist, if my sister decides to be *out of hand*. His words, not mine.

He's reminding me more and more of a crime boss rather than a senator as he gets older. When he initially became interested in a political position, it was all about helping people and our community. With each year that passes and new office he seeks, it seems to become less and less about anyone other than himself.

I shouldn't complain. His choices have offered me many opportunities for financial stability as an adult, as well as a comfortable lifestyle when I was younger. After being away for so long on the road away from him, and then being around the Royal Bastards MC, my eyes have started to open whether I wanted them to or not. I'm seeing things for what they really are, for the first time in my adult life. I've been kept cooped up in this tight-knit bubble of security my entire life, believing I knew what living was about, when I honestly had no idea.

The private jet behind me shields any warmth from the sun and a chill spreads over my skin. This could go either way with Ripper and my father. I know he's brought the cash he's promised, and that's a start. I thought Ripper would be coming with Madison alone, but from the sounds of it, I know it's not only him. The bikers round the bend, the small hill no longer providing any type of shield from the five loud motorcycles. He's brought a small army—five men in his club is equal to ten or fifteen regular men.

I was under the impression Madison would be riding along with Ripper, but I see her snuggled up behind his VP,

Blow. She's got her face tucked into his shoulder, not paying any attention as to where they are. The moment she glances up, she's going to be in for one jarring surprise. I wonder what he told her to get her on the motorcycle with him. It's so windy out today, it can't be much fun. I'd probably be hiding my face as well to keep my eyes from watering in that much wind.

My father and Ripper are complete opposites in every way and that has me on edge. My dad's the epitome of wealth and carries himself every bit as a senator of his state. He screams money all the way from his perfectly trimmed hair to his Italian leather loafers. I should've guessed that Ripper wouldn't be coming alone, knowing who my father is. While my dad thinks he can do what he wants, Ripper is the embodiment of true power. He has no laws, no rules to follow. He's an outlaw one percenter and that means he has nothing to lose. If my father has any sense at all, he won't seek to throw his weight around with the MC.

The powerful, loud machines come to a rumbling stop, and I can't stop myself from staring. The club is a force to be reckoned with as they climb off, clad in black leathers. I recognize Blow, Powerhouse, and Plague, alongside Ripper, but there's one other, big, ominous looking fellow. He's got dark wavy hair to his shoulders, muscles stacked on muscles and a mean glare that's blacker than his wavy locks. He's the type of man that horror stories are made from. There's no doubt in my mind that I would've been intimidated beyond belief had he been at the clubhouse either time I was there.

The guys kick their stands down, and my sister yells in protest as she finally realizes what's about to happen. Blow climbs off his bike, grabbing her to him, walking her toward the private jet. He nuzzles into her, whispering things none of us are privy to hear. She fights him, but her tiny frame is no match against his blunt strength. Blow's not a very big man, probably average, but Madison is petite. She's always been the smallest in our family and Blow dwarfs her as well.

Ripper meets my stare, keeping our gazes locked as they all come to a stop in front of me. "Gem," he greets with his signature throaty rasp. I've noticed it only sounds like that when it comes to the nickname that he's given me. He flicks his intelligent hazel orbs over my thin blouse and business skirt. He's never seen me in my work clothes before now; he's always gotten the relaxed version of me. Especially when he sneaks into my hotel room at night, I'm barely wearing anything at all, eager for his touch.

"Ripper," the road name leaves me on a breath and then two security men are coming down the stairs, my father following behind. He's got two others behind him and one on the plane for backup My own detail stands beside me, not that eight men could protect us from the Royal Bastards. I know better. These guys would never fight fair if it came down to it, and they'd chew through the security guys with bullets like they were an appetizer. The MC takes whatever they want and, in this case, it's cold hard cash for my younger, rebellious sister. Madison's fortunate. Another club could've gotten ahold of her and she may've not been as lucky to make it out of this unscathed.

"Ripper?" My father scans the guys until he lands on the president standing near me. There's no way you can misinterpret who's the leader here. He wears it like an invisible crown.

Ripper nods, appearing stony and intimidating.

"My daughter says you have something to speak with me about...a favor of sorts?"

"I do," Ripper confirms, holding his hand out for my father to shake.

I'd begged my dad to hear him out. Thankfully, he seems to be taking my request seriously. He shakes the biker's hand, offering him a nod. The move sets me at ease, thankful my father isn't rebuking the idea immediately.

"We can walk and talk, if you'd prefer?" my father suggests, and my eyes shoot to Ripper, silently begging him to be on his best behavior. I'd never want to change the stubborn man. I only want him to have a fair shot at getting what he desires.

He acquiesces, and they veer off to the right. Blow picks up his flank and a guard does the same for my father. I watch as Powerhouse securely holds my sister to him. He's careful not to hurt her, while telling her to be a good girl and do as she's told. Little does he know, my sister has never done what she was supposed to. I certainly don't expect her to start now, either.

"You're a bitch, you know that?" Madison says to me as tears streak down her cheeks. Of course, she acts like this is my fault, and she hates me for it. Never mind that she's the one who ran away and scared us all half to death like some unruly teenager. She won't take responsibility for any of it. She never has in the past.

"You should've called, then maybe you could've worked something out with Dad. This isn't my fault."

She scoffs and rolls her eyes, glaring at me as if I'm the filth beneath her shoe. "Give me a fucking break! You know he would've sent the hounds, regardless. He always does."

"Maybe you shouldn't have left in the middle of the night then!" I scream in return, losing my temper. She's so selfish. Doesn't she realize that she's not the only one who bears this responsibility? I'm just as stuck as she is, damn it! Besides, I was just as worried about her too, and let's not forget our poor mother who Dad likes to keep everything from. Her behavior wasn't fair to any of us, yet she wants to place the blame all on me. She's lost it if she believes I'll accept that burden as well.

"I'm a grown woman! You sold me out, you fucking kiss ass!" she shrieks in return.

"Your language has certainly gotten more colorful this time around. This is why he treats you like a child, because you act like one. Excuse me for being worried about you!" Tears prick at the back of my eyes, but I won't allow them to fall.

This is the thanks I get for searching for her for months. She doesn't deserve my tears right now. She's never been happy to come home, but she'd always given in as soon as I've had a chance to really speak to her. This time, though, she's treating me like I'm the Antichrist—as if I'm as bad as our controlling father. The last thing I desire is influence over her life. I only want her safety, for Christ's sake.

She wails into Powerhouse's massive chest, sobbing and calling out brokenly for Blow. She sounds like a little girl who's lost her mother—it's a bit heartbreaking, to be honest. The brawny sergeant at arms wraps her up, shushing her, cooing like she's a fragile being. The entire scene is bizarre, and if my father witnesses her acting like this, he's really going to freak out and make sure she doesn't have a chance to leave again. She'll be married the moment we touch down at home to some country club prepster, knocked up by next week, and placed on a steady supply of Prozac as soon as the kid leaves her womb. If she knew what was good for her, she'd be rational about her behavior. Has she learned nothing from me being trustworthy and devoted to our father? In doing so, he's given me more freedom then she's ever had.

The security guys around us act as if nothing is going on, and it irks me like no other. How can they be so blind? I know they're paid to be discreet, but I'd at least be asking if this was legal.

"Calm down, you're only making this worse than what it could be." I attempt to break through to Madison, but you'd think I was speaking to a wall. She doesn't even acknowledge me. She pretends I'm not here, just like the security guys. She's really gone off the deep end this time around, and I know my father won't take to that very well.

He craves stability and a good image, and she's defying all of that at the moment. On the upside, my father will be too distracted with Madison to pay attention to me. After all this, less attention sounds like a blessing.

I wish I knew how to help Madison, but I'm at a loss. There's only so much I can make happen, unfortunately. While my parents are wealthy and powerful in a sense, depending on which circle they're pushing their weight around in, I don't have the same luxury. My parents' money and father's title is theirs alone. It doesn't help me past getting a decent job or an occasional favor. My sister is on her own with this and I hate that.

I love my father, I really do, but I'm beginning to realize just how much he cages us up. It's not only my sister and me, but my mom too. Only she doesn't fight it. She sneaks around him to get information, but overall, she keeps the peace. Until recently, I'd never realized that I'd been doing the same thing in my own way. Madison's the only one in our family who's repeatedly stood up to him for what she wants.

I used to see her as young and immature, but that's not the case at all. She's brave, and the fact that she's willing to give up everything to find her happiness—to fight for it—has me in awe of her. I've been jaded my entire life, believing that I was the one being a role model for her. When in reality, I should've been taking a page from her book about independence.

"I'm sorry," I manage to whisper in her direction, watching as my father and Ripper begin their stroll back toward the private jet and motorcycles. She stares at me with such devastation, that I can't help but feel a touch of hate bloom in my chest. *What have I done?* I think, but I know the answer to my own question. I can see it plain as day...I've clipped her wings.

The two men come to a stop, sandwiched between my sister and me. I look to them both for any signs that they've reached a mutual deal, or God forbid, the opposite. Ripper had wanted more, though I'm not exactly sure what that was or what it'd entail. Whatever happened between them has things moving so quickly that my mind begins to spin, not knowing what to think.

My father calls for one of his guys and gestures in the direction of Madison. Ripper nods at Powerhouse, and the giant SAA immediately follows the silent order to hand my sister over. Madison fights like a hellcat, screaming and clinging to Powerhouse. She doesn't realize that unless the MC steps in to protect her, nothing will stop my father from putting her on that plane. She's too weak compared to these men and given that she's been doing her fair share of drugs, she's thinner than her usual tiny self.

My father jerks his cell from his inside breast pocket, pressing a speed dial. The person on the other end must answer instantly as he barks, "Marissa!" That one word is all I need to hear to know what's about to happen.

An older, dark haired woman dressed business casual descends the jet's stairs with grace. I recognize her immediately as my father's personal doctor. She's with him at all times when he's busy campaigning to make sure he remains as healthy as possible. The traveling, germs, weather, and everything else combined takes a serious toll on the body.

"Please," he waves toward my sister.

Marissa reaches into her slacks, coming back with a shot. She plucks the plastic protector off the needle and adjusts the plunger.

"I hate you all!" Madison shrieks in outrage, vibrating with fury.

Marissa coos, attempting to come off as soothing. "Shh, darling, this will help you relax. We don't want you to hurt yourself."

Powerhouse and my father's man both struggle to hold my sister still for the doctor. Marissa somehow squeezes in, sinking the shot into my sister's thigh. Madison wails during the entire process, and my stomach spins with unease, making me want to puke. None of this should've ever happened.

One quick glance at Blow shows he's about to lose it himself. He won't do anything until Ripper gives him the okay, though. I think that's the only thing saving anyone from him right now—his respect and loyalty for his president.

My sister grows quiet within moments, her body becoming limp. Powerhouse looks to Ripper before handing her over. Once he has the okay from his prez, Madison is exchanged and is instantly carried to the jet. Marissa follows behind. She'll monitor my sister, checking her vitals and such once they get her laid down on the plane. I know

Madison will be taken care of, but it still has my heart racing for her. I hate that this happened and especially like this. My stubborn younger sister will hold a grudge against me for who knows how long.

The tears I'd been fighting trail down my cheeks. It makes me sick seeing my sister so distraught, and knowing I'm partially responsible for setting this exchange up claws up my insides. I'm overfilled with guilt and turmoil.

My father steps to me, drawing me into his arms. His spicy aftershave that I've sought comfort in so many times in the past, only makes me feel more nauseated. I can't believe everything went this far today. It's crushing to process. I'm in shock that he took it to this level. If she wanted to stay so badly, why didn't he offer up security and just let her have her way? It doesn't fit his narrative, but when is it ever going to be too much to him?

"I'll make sure Madison gets the help she needs. Marissa will take good care of her. Once your sister is back around your mother, she'll come to her senses. Don't you worry about this anymore, honey."

I nod, sniffling. I don't believe that, though—not anymore. I won't say it aloud after witnessing my sister get drugged to stop fighting for her freedom. I could be next at this rate, and that thought absolutely terrifies me. The person I've believed in just showed his true colors, and I can no longer place my trust in him. That revelation is life altering. I've always been a daddy's girl; now, I can't stand the sight of him.

He pulls back, holding my shoulders to meet my teary gaze. He offers me a smile, the kind one he'd often only share with me in the midst of his busy days. It always made me believe that I was his favorite. I was stupid. "Ripper tells me you've been enjoying it here. That's good to hear, honey."

I bite my cheek. There's a lump in my throat that feels as big as a baseball. I offer a silent nod, not wanting to upset him and taste the repercussions. I've always thought that I knew my father completely, but apparently, I know nothing.

He squeezes my shoulders affectionately, the smile lines around his eyes crinkling. "After so much traveling, you deserve a chance to relax. I was planning on us having a celebration when you came home, but Ripper made another suggestion."

I can feel the man in question's gaze burning into me, but I don't dare break eye contact with my father. If I show him any disrespect, he shuts down. He's been like that for as long as I can remember. "How thoughtful," I offer, managing to conjure up a placating smile.

"Indeed. He's offered to host you here for a while longer. Only if you'd like to stay, that is."

"I would love to. There's so much in central Texas that I've yet to see. This sunshine is a nice changeup compared to home too."

He nods, acting as if he'd thought the same thing. It's all lies. Everything is a lie. How could I have been so blind before to not see it?

"Ripper has agreed to allow Richardson to stay back with you. We have an understanding that the MC will assist in protecting you." He wags his finger to implement his words. "Don't leave the safety he's offering, or I'll be forced to send your team back."

It takes everything in me to not jump up and down and squeal in excitement. I don't know what type of voodoo magic Ripper managed to work over my father, but he'll be getting his cock sucked later for it.

"How generous." I flick my eyes to Ripper's momentarily. "Thank you."

He nods, wearing a haughty smirk. *The cocky bastard.* I don't care, though; he can be a bit conceited after working out a deal with my father for me to stay here. The only thing that could make it any better would be Madison remaining here with me. That will never happen though, and I know better than to ask.

Ripper murmurs, "It's nothing. I'm glad we could work something out that'll make us all happy."

My father nods along, like a life-sized bobble head. "I hate to cut this short, honey, but I need to get your sister home and back on the right track. I have a feeling this time will take longer than the last. I wish she were more like you," he confesses, making me uncomfortable. I'm standing here wishing I were more like her in the courage and independence department.

I lean in to give him a squeeze and then step out of his hold, wanting him to leave as soon as humanly possible. "Have a safe flight."

"Will do and we'll speak soon. Love you, Alice."

"Love you too," I reply automatically and slide another step closer to Ripper. I'm almost in the clear.

I can handle having Richardson here; he doesn't bother me much. He won't be fond of being around Ripper and his MC brothers, but that's not my problem. My father is willingly leaving me with Ripper, so he must've asked for something extensive in return. Frankly, I'm shocked he's allowing me to stay here at all, let alone with the MC. I was expecting him to snub the club and have me on the next flight home, quicker than I could blink. Something extraordinary had to happen between them for me to be remaining in Texas.

I could ask Ripper for more details, but I have a feeling he won't say much, and my father will only lie. That much I'm certain of now. I should probably worry about what my freedom's costing, but at the moment, I can't find it in myself to.

While I'm sad for my sister, I'm grateful I'm not in her shoes. There's no telling what my father has planned for her. Call me heartless, but at some point, I have to think of myself. I was literally traipsing all over the country looking for her. I've done more than what I should've, according to Madison. She wants me to butt out of her life, so that's what I'm going to do.

Richardson falls in beside me as I turn in the direction of the Cadillac. My belongings are in the trunk, along with Richardson's. I wonder if we'll check back into the same hotel or if we can find one closer to Ripper? That's not up to me, unless I'm paying for it, and my father never mentioned as much. To me, that means he's footing this bill, and after discovering he's not the man I thought he was, I'll take whatever I can get from his pockets. I don't care if that sounds shallow. I'm angry and feel betrayed if I'm being honest with myself.

Ripper growls, "Where do you think you're goin', Gem?"

The deep rasp pulls me from my thoughts. I spin around to him, my brows lifting. "I'm going to the car. We've got to check back into the hotel and put our things in our rooms."

He chuckles, adopting that sexy grin I enjoy so much, while swaggering over to me. He stops less than a foot away and shakes his head. "Oh, no, babe."

"No?" I cock a brow, confused. *I thought I was staying here.*

"Mm, you're coming home with me. Didn't you hear your pops? You're staying with me and my club. Same as ol' boy, here." He tilts his head in the direction of Richardson. My mouth falls open. I definitely wasn't expecting this turn of events. "Your security is my motherfuckin' priority now, not any hired suits. I agreed to him." He chin-lifts to my personal bodyguard. "Staying as a courtesy to your father. He can follow in the cage. You ride with me on my bike, and that goes for all times, babe."

Richardson moves to protest, but I hold my hand up, stopping him before he starts any trouble. "I've never ridden on a motorcycle."

"There's a first time for everything. Hike that skirt up on your sexy thighs, wrap them gorgeous legs around me, and hold the fuck on. There ain't much else to it." He winks, placing his palm out to me.

I smile, my cheeks pink at all the compliments he managed to work into his brief instructions. "Don't threaten me with a good time." I lay my hand in his, allowing him to take me where he wants.

I can hear Richardson protesting all the way to the bikes, and I can't help but laugh. He eventually takes the hint as I climb on the motorcycle behind Ripper and wrap my arms tightly around his middle. Richardson takes off in a jog to the car as the thunder of the roaring engines consumes the air.

I manage to get off a quick wave to my father's plane, as I know he's probably fuming at seeing me like this, then I hold on to the delicious man before me. I'm ready for the ride of my life, and there's no doubt in my mind, Ripper's the man to give it to me.

Chapter 12

> Don't try to win over the haters.
> You are not a jackass whisperer.
> - Brene Brown

Ripper

The agreement

We managed to strike a deal, her father and me. It took a bit of finesse, but I was able to get what I wanted out of it overall, and in the end, so will he. I think back to how we'd walked until we came to the old ramshackle of an airport building. The private owner left the dilapidated brick structure in place and built another not too far away. I guess they weren't willing to put the energy into it when they could just forget about the place and toss money at something new. Typical rich people, in my personal opinion.

"*My daughter says you have something to speak to me about.*" He turns to me. I don't catch much of a father-daughter resemblance in his face, so Alice must look more like her mother.

Senator Compton isn't at all what I was anticipating. I've seen him on the billboards, sure, but he's different in person. His pictures show him with rich chestnut hair, not the faded gray brown mix he's currently sporting. He also seems bigger in the photos, livelier. I'm thinking maybe that was the extra ten pounds the camera puts on, though. This man before me looks every bit like he could be Alice's father. Older, rich, well dressed, and non-threatening. If it weren't for his political ties making him influential, I'd swoop Alice up and keep her to myself, without ever acknowledging this uptight bastard.

I accept his statement with a head tilt. "That's right. I asked Alice to arrange this meeting between us."

"Well, shall we get to it? I'm a busy man."

"Yep," I grunt, biting back a retort that he has a full staff to do every fucking thing for his pampered ass. I'm the one putting in actual work to make shit happen, not that he'd know anything about a hard day's work. He's not blue collar; I doubt he's ever been.

Alice had prewarned me that being rude or having an attitude with her father is not the way to get him to listen. She said if I go in headstrong then he'll shut me out right *away. Stubborn and opinionated is my everyday persona, so this is a stretch, but I'm giving it a shot.*

"I appreciate you taking the time, Senator Compton. I'll get right to it. I need a favor."

His dull gray eyebrows rise as he folds his arms across his chest. "Already? The money isn't enough for returning my daughter to me?" *He acts like I'm the one putting him out, when in reality, I'm doing him a fucking favor. I didn't have to make this any of my business. Maddy is a grown woman. If she wants to strip, snort, and fuck, who am I to tell her no? If it weren't for this prick having the cash, the club wouldn't have wasted the time on any of this.*

"It is. I figured it wouldn't hurt to ask for more, however."

"What can I do for you? I make no promises, but if it's within my reach, I'll see what I can do."

"I have a brother being held on charges of possession."

I see the judgment fill his eyes immediately. Thank fuck I never had to deal with my ol' man looking at me like this. I'd have put a bullet in him if that was the case. I got the lucky end of the stick with my pops, as he's one hundred percent supported me in the club life. He wished I'd have pledged to his club, but he got over it. This fucker here, has me realizing why Alice is so punctual and uptight. She's a good girl, a rule follower—she was until she met me, anyhow.

I push on before he has a chance to interrupt and shoot me down already. "He was on a job for me, and now he's looking at doing a few years' time for something he never should've been arrested for. If you're able to get him let off, it could look good for you with the cannabis voters. I read that your state is attempting to make recreational use legal. This could show your voters that you're serious about taking that step."

He hums, silently thinking it over. I've caught him off guard with my request. The fucker's probably in shock over the fact I read, but little does he know, aptitude has never been a struggle for me. I didn't choose the club life because I had no other choice; I chose it because I love it.

The senator looks me over, clearly pondering my request. He must've believed I was going to blackmail him, not offer up an opportunity. It's in disguise of a favor to the club, but it works, nonetheless.

"It'd be a far reach for me," he finally sputters. I'm not sure I believe him though. "I'd have to call in multiple favors, as I've never spoken to your governor, nor anyone else who has the power to make those doors open in Texas. For the right incentive, I may be willing to go out of my way to see it happen. Tell me, Ripper, to what lengths does your club go to-to solve another man's problems?"

"Depends." I shrug with the reply, leaning against the brick to help block the serious wind gusts we're having today.

I'm surprised the plane was able to land here in this shit without any issues. I sure as fuck wouldn't want to fly around in it—riding was bad enough. The gusts were pushing us all over the fucking place. If there weren't six of us leaving the club, I'd have rolled up in a truck and avoided the nuisance altogether. If it weren't for the incentive of a big payday, I'd have fucked off altogether.

"On what?"

"Well, the payout...if there is any. It'd be contingent on the possible blowback, as well as the level of difficulty. Finally, it'd have to be voted on by my brothers and me. If it seems like something we can handle, we don't mind getting our hands dirty to solve some problems for folks. Hell, we may even enjoy it." I wink at that last little dig. He needs to know he's not shaking me up in the least bit with his shady requests. I can be a fucking monster if I'm pushed enough.

His lips tip into a sinister grin. "That's what I was hoping you'd say. This particular request has to be handled delicately. No one can ever link it back to me, in any way."

I nod, promising, "I can make sure that happens." My brow wrinkles as I become more serious, and my voice lowers an octave as I declare adamantly, "Depending on what it is and what we get out of it."

"I need someone to disappear."

"Okay." I draw the word out, needing more than that. Does he want me to kidnap someone or kill them? And is this personal, does it need to be simple or a fucking bloodbath of torture?

"Forever."

"Ah, and would I know who this somebody is?"

"Most likely not, unless you follow the elections in my state."

"Then that would be a no. I don't know any politicians from that part of the country aside from you, and I don't want to."

He offers me a slimy smile. "That's another good answer. If I can get your buddy released, would you be willing to make this problem I have go away?"

"That's a steep request, and a lot more risk than what you'd be doing for me."

"I can pay. Name your price, and I'll see to it that you get whatever you need to complete this task."

"I've got money, and even more now that you've traded with my club for Maddy. I don't usually deal in human flesh, but in this case, it worked out well for both of us."

He releases a tense breath, his gaze skirting around before trying again. "All right, then, what would you want in return? I'm sure we can come to some sort of an agreement. I'm a man with many means."

It's my turn to grin, and I do so cockily. I have him right where I want him. He's requesting something significant, and whether he gives me what I want and we go through with it or not, I have his ass. I could bluff and tell him I've recorded this conversation, and I plan to leak it to the press. I would never outright record a deal, but he doesn't know that. He knows nothing about me. There's more than one angle for me to work now, to get what I desire. He's an amateur at this shit compared to us, fucking outlaws who've lived our lives doing whatever the fuck we want, following no laws or rules.

"Alice and I have become...friends," I commence, not wanting to tarnish her in his judgmental eyes.

He stares at me with skepticism and repeats, "Friends?" The old fucker can't seem to come to terms with why his daughter would be mixed up with someone like me. I want to come out with it and tell him it's because of my enormous cock and the way I fuck her, but I doubt that'd win him over anytime soon.

"Yep. Turns out she likes Texas a whole helluva lot and isn't ready to go back home. She wasn't sure how to break it to you and was certain you'd be against it. But, now that we've met and we're also friends, I figure you won't have a problem if she sticks around for a bit."

His Adam's apple bobs as he swallows tightly. "A- and how do I know you'd let her come home when she's ready?"

I shrug. Maybe I would, maybe I wouldn't. "Guess you'd just have to trust me, like I'd be trusting you with these other plans. You let Alice hang around back here, and I know you'll keep good on your part of the bargain. It'll also give me peace of mind, that you won't grow a conscious and contact this enemy of yours to warn him. It wouldn't be the first time a man went soft and hung himself out to dry. Which, by the way, is a death sentence in its own accord."

"You're, uh, not very trusting, I take it?" Suddenly he's looking nervous. The reality of what's happening and how immoral I am must've finally sunk home for him. I'm a fucking killer, and now he knows it. The funniest part of all, is that I'm going to get what I desire no matter what he wants to do. Like I said before, I have multiple ways to work my angle now, thanks to his stupidity.

"Nah, this isn't my first rodeo. I make my living by breaking the rules and doing whatever the fuck I choose to. The real kicker is, I have a club full of motherfuckers just as crazy, if not batshit crazier than me."

His hands begin to shake. He attempts to hide them by tucking them into his slate colored slacks pockets, but I catch on before he can. I fucking love knowing he's scared of me and my brothers. "If that's the case, how will I know that Alice won't be harmed in any of this?" It's a reasonable question, and I commend him for not being so narrow-minded to not consider the safety of his daughter. He must not be a total fucking failure if he's got enough sense to ask on her behalf.

"That's one thing I will give you my word on, here and now," I stress. There's no way I'd allow her to be collateral damage in any of this shit. Our agreement is business between him and me. Alice won't be the wiser, nor would she pay for any of his fuckups.

"You'll keep her safe?" he probes, needing confirmation.

"Of course, and better yet, I'll make sure she's happy too. If at any time she wants to leave, she can walk right out my doors and you can send whoever the fuck you want to pick her up." I leave out the bit that I may not let her go in the end and kill any motherfucker who attempts to take her before I'm finished with her. I'm growing more possessive of *her as the days pass, and that isn't good for anyone trying to take her from me.*

"I feel like I should warn you. She has security detail for a reason. There've been threats."

"What kind of threats?" *My muscles tense at the thought of anyone touching that sweet, caring woman. I can't imagine someone being her enemy. The only thing she's guilty of is having a heart too big.*

"Against my family. One in specific was aimed at Alice, promising to hurt her. I've had this particular team with her night and day. I'm fearful that whoever's been threatening her will, at the very least, kidnap her...if not kill her."

This stupid motherfucker was careless enough to send her out on a wild goose chase all to safeguard his fucking image, when she could've been killed? Right there tells me all I need to know about Senator Compton. I fucking hate him, and if it weren't for Alice, I'd put a bullet in his head too.

"Then, this is a blessing in disguise for you, Senator. She couldn't be any safer than in my club, surrounded by ruthless men." *And, if I decide to put my patch on her, anyone endangering her well-being would be a direct threat to the entire club. My club would mow them over in a heartbeat.*

"Why would they protect her? They don't owe her their allegiance."

"No, they don't. However, they're steadfast when it comes to me, and in case you haven't noticed, I'm the *president of my charter. Everyone answers to me. They're loyal to me. That protection extends to anyone else I need it to. If I ask them to guard Alice for me, they will with their life. That security detail you set up for her, couldn't get near her when she was in my clubhouse asking about Maddy. One person hunting her down, or even a few individuals, wouldn't get anywhere near her. Especially not to hurt her, and if I ever caught wind of them attempting it, I can promise you, they'd die. I'd make it a slow, painful death, while they begged for mine and her forgiveness."*

This sort of thing would scare off most men, but for me it does the opposite. It makes me crave Alice even more than I already do. I want to hurt any motherfucker who comes near her with evil intent. Then, I want her to watch me do it, so she knows damn well she's got a man who can protect her. She'll never feel unsafe again, so long as I'm by her side. I'll make sure of it.

"It's settled, then." He holds his hand out for me to shake. "We have a deal as long as I have your vote."

I roll my eyes at his pun. Fuckin' idiot. "Alice has my vote. That being said, it will extend in your favor. I'll be in contact to set everything up. I suggest you take my call when the phone rings. I don't give a fuck what you're in the middle of; I'm not the type of man who waits."

He swallows tightly, his Adam's apple bobbing as he nods his agreeance. "You have my word."

"Then you have mine," I finish, leaving him to walk behind me. I've gotten what I wanted. Now I need to get the fuck out of here and put Alice on my bike and in my bed.

Church

"We've got shit to discuss, brothers," I begin Church by stating the obvious. Lately, it seems like we're cooped up in this room all the fucking time. "You're aware I met with that senator yesterday."

They nod, staring me down. I know their curiosity has been eating them up. I go on, relaying the gist of the deal that Senator Compton and I struck. I don't know why I hold back, but I avoid mentioning that the arrangement includes Alice's brief taste of freedom. The club has to be on board with the plan of action, or it'll never work out how I want it too. I also need something significant to hang over the senator in case he ever tries to take Alice away from me.

Whiskey speaks up in agreement. "It'll be worth it, bringing Baker home where he belongs."

Angel scowls. "It's a risk. We'd be in other MC and gang territory, and that could backfire."

Powerhouse gestures to our enforcer, stating, "Angel is right. Not only that, but we'd be reaching into politics, and it could incite blowback on the other charters—not just ours. The Royal Bastards linked to a senator and murder would send the media into an uproar. It does go against code, to a degree."

Plague glances at me with confusion. "Code?"

I nod.

He goes on, scoffing. "We may've said that shit in the beginning when we pledged, but you know as well as I do, it means fuck all. We do what we want. Hell, we always have…"

"I know, but this could bite us in the ass if we're not cautious. If we go through with it, we have no room for any fuckups. No one can catch light of our hit."

"Look, Prez, this isn't the motherfuckin' girl scouts. The other charters are into some twisted shit, just as we are, they gotta be."

I keep my thoughts to myself on his statement. I agree with him, but by being the president of this charter, it would damn near be blasphemy. If I agree out loud and the wrong person were to overhear it, the repercussions could hit me hard. Take Rancid, for example. I repeat, "We move forward, we risk inciting unrest, *but* if we're careful, we stay under the radar and make a lot of money."

Blow breaks his silence, staring me down. He steeples his hands under his chin, muttering, "And you get to keep her."

"What?" I question, taken off guard. I fucking heard him, but how does he know that part of the deal? That conversation was supposed to be between Senator Compton and me, no one else.

"I heard you on the other side of the busted ass door. I was waiting for you and your conversation was clear as day." He's got all the brothers attention now, as they jerk their heads back and forth between us. This is exactly what I didn't want. Our discussion went from the job to my personal shit.

Fuck!

"Who—"

"Else heard?" he finishes for me. "No one. I made sure his suit was away from the crumbling bricks. He may've overheard your voices, but there's no way he could've made out the words like I did. The wind along that dilapidated building masked a lot of what you were saying."

Releasing a tense breath, I say, "All right, then." The other brothers stare curiously, obviously not knowing what the fuck we're talking about. They trust me completely. They always have, without question. I have to tell them everything. I owe them that much if we're going to put this into play and possibly get popped for it. "If we do this, the senator will back off Alice and me." I come clean to the table about the rest of the deal I orchestrated.

Whiskey rasps, "Then that's settled."

"What is?"

He gestures in my direction. "You put that woman on the back of your bike. If this is what we gotta do so you have your woman, then so be it." He shrugs it off like the answer is simple.

"Brothers, you would risk this for me?" I question and they all immediately move to agree.

I'm a cold bastard, but this is enough to give me the feels. My brothers would risk the wrath of the other charters coming down on us, of the media possibly catching fire to our plans...all for my happiness with a woman I've known for less than a month. This is what true brotherhood is about, having each other's backs, even when you have the option to pick another route.

Angel growls, "Fuckin' claim her." And it's as simple as that. I know what I have to do.

Chapter 13

> Isn't it funny how day by day
> nothing changes but when you look
> back everything is different.
> C.S. Lewis

Alice

"They're doing that right here?" I can't help but lean in and quietly ask. I'm snuggled up next to Ripper, enjoying his camaraderie with his brothers in their club's bar. The big burly guy who I discovered is surprisingly called Angel, is enjoying some female companionship. I'm all for it, but what shocked me, is that he unzipped his pants and the woman immediately dropped to the floor, her face in his lap. Her head quickly begins to bob, and I catch glimpses of Angels tan veiny cock as she goes. I'm trying not to stare, but it's hard not to when it's right in front of you on display.

Ripper follows my stare, chuckling. "Angel prefers having an audience."

My eyes widen as I meet his sparkling gaze, catching on to what he means. Of course, he thinks my reaction is hilarious. "Does this, uh, sort of thing happen often then?"

He shrugs. "Often enough. All the brothers have had their cock sucked in this room at some point."

I gasp. "No one minds it? Please tell me that lemon scent is disinfectant and not anything else."

He smirks, leaning in to press an amused kiss to my forehead. It's sweet and has me relaxing again. "Here, the brothers are free from judgment. They may catch some shit from us, but we accept them for who they are."

"That's very admirable of you," I offer, respecting them for their acceptance.

"Not really, Gem. These men are my brothers; we're the family we choose. If I wasn't going to accept them and have their backs, I wouldn't be here." He sends me a pointed glance, and I take the hint. If I want to stick around and be with him, I need to accept these guys too. I may not agree with everything or partake in what they do, but I need to let go of any judgments I may harbor. That will be hard...I won't deny it. Coming from a somewhat conservative lifestyle, the MC is everything I didn't grow up around. I guess it all boils down to how much I want to be with

Ripper. He's a packaged deal—the MC being his counterpart.

"I respect that, and I like to think I'm somewhat open-minded. I won't judge, but it'll take some getting used to."

He nods. "I get it. Hell, maybe you'd like to join in sometime?" He casts me a wink, his white teeth on display with his signature grin. The man is all-natural charm, even though he comes off as a prick most the time. He's one of those guys that no matter how hard you try to be annoyed with, you can't.

I roll my eyes, throwing back a little bit of sass. "Don't go holding your breath."

Richardson appears more than interested, though, I think to myself, as I watch his attention glued to the free show in front of us all. We've been staying here at the clubhouse for two weeks now. My father swooped in and quickly departed, leaving me with minimal restrictions. It's the first time for a lot of things for me. I'm trying not to go crazy with the loosened leash, as I love the feeling of freedom more than I ever expected and am dreading the moment he takes it away.

My bodyguard doesn't seem to mind the freedom either. Each day he comes out of his room looking a bit more rugged. At first, it was the suits. That changed within a few days into jeans and a plain T-shirt. I notice he's not even wearing tennis shoes any longer, but a pair of boots like the rest of the guys around here and a leather belt to match. This week he's gone as far as to not shave each day and has a dusting of hair over his face. It's a different look for him, but he seems to be enjoying it. It's like knowing the usual Richardson and then also the undercover version. Most of the MC brothers ignore him, although I've caught him talking to Wrench several times. I'm glad he's found someone here to interact with and isn't miserably alone.

"Speaking of holding our breath, when can we go swimming?"

His brow wrinkles as he tilts his head to look me over. "It's too cold for that shit."

"I meant in an indoor pool."

He shakes his head, driving his point in. "Babe, once it warms up, I'll take you to some real swimming spots."

"That sounds wonderful," I reply, also noting that he said when it warms up. Does that mean he plans on keeping me around for a lot longer than a few weeks' time? As much as I don't want to leave, I figured my visit here was starting to run out. Ripper and I have a good time together, and while I want more with him, I can't imagine he'd want me in the same way. We're completely different. That has to make him hesitate, I'd think.

Richardson interrupts our conversation. "I can search around for an indoor pool that's safe enough for you to swim your laps."

Ripper pins his gaze on my guard, shooting him daggers. "The fuck you just say?"

Richardson's brow rises. He retorts, "I work for Alice, not for you."

Ripper stands, and I tug his wrist to me, not wanting him to go after my guard. "You're in my clubhouse, and if what I've heard is correct, that you may be a prospect candidate, then you'll learn to shut the fuck up when it comes to my word around here."

Richardson stands up as well and I groan to myself. This isn't going to end well. He points in my direction and I cringe. "This may be your club, but I'm here for her."

"She's *my* motherfuckin' woman!" Ripper roars, stunning the club into silence. I'm panting, staring up at him, at his declaration. He glowers at my guard, stating, "She's *mine*. If I tell her to wait, it's for a fuckin' reason. You defy me, *boy*, and I'll bury your punk ass."

Richardson is in his midtwenties, so Ripper threw that bit in to chafe him on an experience level. I'm not fond of what's happening, but I'm at a loss on what I should do. If I come between them, then Ripper may think I'm taking Richardson's side. If I stand up to Richardson, then I'll be discrediting his commitment to me.

Did I have to pick the most stubborn man in Texas to start falling for? And what happens to my security if I do stick with Ripper? Richardson is someone I'd consider a friend and loyalty has to count for something where friendship is concerned. And what did Ripper mean about him prospecting? Could that really be true?

I speak up, asking, "Ah, Richardson? Is that true? Is joining the Royal Bastards something you could see yourself doing?"

He meets my curious stare and concedes. We're not super close, but I can't help but feel a bit upset that he didn't mention anything before. We've had many hours in the car while searching for Madison, that we've broached the surface on things. I think of him in a brotherly sense and as a colleague. He glances at the members positioned around me and declares, "If you're making this your permanent home, then I was planning on doing the same."

My eyes are wide, my chest carved open by his loyalty. This man would sacrifice his home and his potential happiness to have my back. That truly means something. "Thank you for that, but I don't know if Ripper and I want the same future." I can't believe I'm having this conversation openly in front of the club, but if it staves off a fight between these guys, then so be it. I'll swallow my pride and lay it out in the open.

Whiskey argues, "The prez said you're his. Don't see anything else to discuss about it."

My lips turn up at his quick rationalization. The older fellow is never one to hold back on his opinion about anything. I've come to learn that Ripper respects him a great deal because of it. Personally, I enjoy his touch of honesty and bluntness. His comment is enough to set the brothers at ease and several chuckle with the tension leaving the air.

"He did say that, didn't he?" I meet the wise man's stare, catching the twinkle in his eyes. He must approve, and that makes me feel pretty good inside to have a brother's approval for their leader.

"Damn right, I did," Ripper mutters dejectedly, pulling me into his chest.

He doesn't give me a chance to say another word as he plants his lips on mine. He kisses me like a man starved for affection, and I return it with everything I've got. If he's starved, then I'm parched, and he's my water. I've never felt such a resilient tug toward a man as I do with him. He's not anyone I'd ever pictured having in my life, but I don't care. He makes me happy, he makes me feel free and desired, and that's a heady combination for a woman not used to being in control of her own life.

He draws back, sucking my bottom lip for a beat before finally releasing the tender flesh. His forehead tenderly leans against mine, his nose grazing my own as he stares at me intently. "Let me take you to my room, Gem. I wanna make you feel good."

I flick my eyes at the members behind him, then at the darkened clubhouse. There're lights on behind the bar and around the room, but they're dimmed. With the night sky in full force, it brought a shadow of privacy we don't usually have during the day. I press a chaste kiss to his lips, pausing to nibble on his plump bottom lip. I suggestively whisper against his mouth, "Or you could take me here."

His head moves to my throat as he tucks closer into me and rasps. "You have any fuckin' idea what that thought does to me?" he growls, sending a shiver of delight through my body. "Every brother in this joint will be jealous of what I have, of what *belongs to me*."

His proclamation has me wanting him to go through with my request even more than I did when I'd said it. I don't know why the idea came to me at all, but it's too late to take it back now. "I don't care about any other person in this room, but you," I manage to gasp out as he bites at the flesh behind my ear.

Ripper's chest rumbles with approval. He likes knowing that I only want him. His beefy arms wrap around me tightly and in the next moment he has me across the room, pressed up against the far wall. The others have the perfect seats to watch him pin me in place, shove my skirt up my hips and press his jean clad cock against my core. "Fuck," he groans. "If you want to go to the room, you tell me now. If you don't say anything, I'm sliding in this pussy here and now."

My chest heaves. I'm panting with the depth of what's happening. His hardness presses into my clit, making me go cross-eyed at the sensation. "Please," escapes me on a whimper. He loves when I ask nicely for his cock.

"Mm, you gonna beg for it, Gem? You start saying please like that, and I'm never taking my cock outta you."

A giggle breaks free. "You say that like it's a bad thing, like it's supposed to be a threat."

"Fuck, babe. Why do you have to be so fuckin' perfect that I don't wanna let you go, hm?"

My head tilts at him going from sexy to demanding to sweet. Yeah, he's a bastard biker, but he has his moments with me. "Don't let me go, Ripper, at least not yet."

He nods. "I can do that," he promises and slides my panties to the side. He works his cock into my opening. I'm scatterbrained. When did he unzip his pants? Or maybe he just shoved them down amid his sweet words? I don't know, nor does it matter. What does, is that I want him an insane amount.

"Stop stalling, Prez," I murmur, and it tips him over the edge. He slams into me, making me call out his name.

The brothers hoot and holler behind us, loving every minute of this. I can't argue; I think it's pretty great myself. My hands move to his chest, wanting to feel his skin, to see it and taste his salty flesh. He has his cut on over his T-shirt, so I know it won't come off right now like I want. The cut is practically sacred to the Royal Bastards. I've learned a lot of little things about the MC and the lifestyle these guys live since coming here. They follow very few rules, but the couple they have, they're devoted to upholding.

"I'll show you stalling, you mouthy woman."

I lean my head back against the wall, closing my eyes and wearing a wide smile. He takes advantage of the position, nipping and sucking on my throat. He knows what it does to me, especially when he's inside my hot center. Having him pressed up against me like this, his frame flexed with his movements is an aphrodisiac in its own. Ripper is full of pent up power and when he's fucking, it's like he can finally unleash some of it.

"Harder," I beg loudly, and his hips piston forward with a jolt. His groin rubs against my pussy in the best type of way. "Oh, yes!" I don't attempt to hold myself back, he deserves to have all of me whether we have an audience or not.

My lids barely part open, but it's enough for me to catch the enforcer watching us while the sweetbutt on her knees continues to suck him off. He must be fond of watching others have sex, as much as he enjoys being observed by an audience. Ripper and I have the entire club's attention, their gazes transfixed on their prez taking me here in the bar this very moment. I've never been so sexually brazen with a man in my life. Still, there's something about Ripper that provokes me to step outside of my ordinarily square box. He makes me want to experience everything, even if it'll possibly make me uncomfortable—he incites me to wake up and live.

"You're mine, Gem. 'Bout time you realized that, babe."

I lean in, pressing my mouth to his flesh with my own personal assault on his neck. Between kisses, I purr, "What's that entail exactly, Ripper?"

"It means that no one else touches you," he breathes out and drives deep into my core. My pussy spasms around his shaft with the formidable onslaught of heavenly sensations. It's too much, and yet, not nearly enough. I want more—always more—of him.

"Oh," I moan, nipping at his earlobe. "I like the sound of that. As long as no one touches you either."

"I don't need anyone else. I only crave you and your creamy cunt," Ripper reassures me, and my stomach twirls.

My heart thuds faster at his implication. I'm on sensory overload, as his cock fills me and his words serenade me.

His fingers trail upward from my hip to pinch my stiff, over sensitized nipple, rendering me to the point I begin to see stars. "Oh, yes!" I howl in bliss, my orgasm beginning to build. My pussy squeezes him with each movement, yearning to hold him deep inside. "You're going to get tired of me," I vow, licking up his salty neck until I move to press my forehead against his. He's peppered with sweat. Surprisingly, it's not off-putting, but rather sexy. His pheromones are all around me, dragging me under his spell until I'm at the point of no return. *Ripper can have me.*

He meets my gaze, all joking and lightheartedness pushed aside, to genuinely state, "Nah, woman. When a brother lays claim, that's it. You're the one who's meant to be on the back of my bike."

His proclamation chokes me up. I'm so turned on and close to my orgasm, that when tears fill my eyes, I'm a hot freaking mess. "Y-you really want me that much?"

His lips fall to mine. He sucks the top into his mouth then releases it to take the bottom and repeat his delightful assault. He can't seem to stop kissing or touching me, and in that aspect, I can't get enough of him either. "I want you somethin' fierce, Gem. I thought you knew that?"

A few droplets crest and tumble down my cheeks. "I'm falling for you," I admit as my pussy squeezes him, and he throbs in response. *It's too soon.* Everything about this screams that it's rushed, but no matter how much I pump the brakes, it just won't slow down.

I merely had two weeks with Ripper before my father came to collect Madison. The first and second week that I came across the cocky biker, he managed to kiss me twice. The end of the second week, he snuck into my hotel room nightly and fucked me into the early morning hours. That lead into the third week, then boom, I was thrust into his life full time. I've been staying at the club for an additional two weeks. We're going on week three here, so that's not even six full weeks we've spent together, and I'm so far gone for this man, I may as well rip my heart out and stomp on it.

If Ripper decides he doesn't want to be with me eventually, I know it'll lead me straight to heartbreak. However, he just admitted that he does crave me like I do him, that he needs me, and he's claiming me as his. Could it really all be that simple? A man and a woman find each other, catch feelings, and decide it's forever? Does that type of relationship even exist in real life?

"Fall harder, Alice," he whispers for my ears only, diving in for another mouthwatering kiss.

My hands rake into his hair. I fist his locks to keep him near, to make this kiss go on forever. He holds me to him—so tightly that it physically hurts, but I don't care. I need it. I crave his touch, no matter what all of this may entail in the end. With the decision made up in my mind already, my orgasm takes over. Pleasure fires through my veins, moans escape through our passion filled embrace.

The sexy, enticing biker clutches onto me intensely, to the point that there'll be bruises peppering my flesh tomorrow. The knowledge that he's marking me up so zealously has me thrusting my pelvis forward to meet his. I bite down on his lower lip savagely, moaning as my peak builds to the max, making me feel delirious.

My intense orgasm drives him to his bursting point. Hot seed shoots from his pulsing length into my pussy, causing mini palpitations to continuously tremble throughout my core. "Ripper!" I scream at the crescendo, both of our orgasms plummeting through us at the same time.

"Fuck!" he growls in response. His rock-hard cock continues to throb, repeatedly filling my core with every drop his heavy sack has to offer. My pussy overfills to the point his thick, creamy cum leaks down my thighs.

"So, so, so good," I pant, dizzily meeting his gaze.

His hazel irises are stormy, filled with unspoken emotions. I know mine are reflecting back the same way…not that I mind. He told me to fall harder. He can't blame me for listening. "I wanna keep you," he declares stubbornly. "This here showed anyone who may've doubted my word, that I mean it. I'd be honored if you'd wear my patch, Gem."

"What does that even mean?" I ask quietly, still lost in the feelings from some of the most intense sex I've ever had before. This guy has no idea what he does to me physically and emotionally.

He carefully draws back, jerking my skirt in place to cover my cum soaked thighs. He moves to fix my blouse for me also, before he goes to tuck his cock back inside his jeans. "Exactly what you think…what I said while we were fucking."

"You don't think it's too soon?" I can hear the guys yelling in the background, but this conversation is far too important to break eye contact and allow them to interrupt us.

He shrugs. "I'm going by what I feel, not by what I think. My heart and my gut tell me you're *it* for me. I'm not trying to scare you, but I want you to know that this is absolutely real to me. After hearing you tell the guys you weren't sure what I wanted, it's pretty fucking imperative that I make myself clear with my intentions."

Biting my inner cheek, I think over what he's saying. No matter how unconventional I'd have thought it to be in the past, this is what I want now. The only problem standing in my way right now is my father. I can't see him accepting Ripper and me as a couple or in any scenario that has us ending up together. Although I was shocked with him allowing me to remain back with Ripper a while longer. I know it doesn't mean it's a permanent thing, when it comes to my father's compliancy though.

"My heart is telling me it wants you too."

"Then what's the issue? I can see it in your eyes...there's something bothering you." He takes a step backward but reaches for my hand. He's always touching me. That's another thing I like. He never makes me feel like I'm putting him out, but that he wants me close by his side.

"You've met my father, Ripper...he's not exactly fond of his daughters having much freedom."

"Mm," he grunts, pulling me away from the wall. He turns around, dropping my hand to tuck me under his arm.

He takes his time with me, striding back to the table with the others. Before we reach them, he says, "You let me worry about the senator, yeah? You just concentrate on relaxing and getting used to the club. If I have any say in how this turns out, this'll be one of your homes. The other will be alone with me, when we're ready for it."

I shoot him a soft look, my lips tilting up. Like I said before, this bastard has his moments. I'll do as he asks, and if my father doesn't eventually concede, I have a feeling that I'll be the next one running away from him.

Chapter 14

*You are either on my side,
by my side, or in my fucking way.
Choose wisely.
- Our Mindful Life*

Ripper

The mark was easy to get to. He's not as well protected as Senator Compton's grown accustomed to being. This idiot merely has a basic security system inside his big ass gated mansion. He doesn't even have cameras; he's making this far too easy on us.

  Once Gem and I had our little talk in the club, I knew I had to get up here and take care of this shit. I need something on her pops to hold him off for good, and murder is just the thing to do it. I'm not planning on letting Alice go back to that overbearing fuck, and if he fights me on it, he'll pay. Of that, I'm certain. I told my woman to let me handle him, and she's agreed. I'm pretty sure she doesn't know what in the hell to do with me, so she just goes with it. It's one of the many things I enjoy about her most—her willingness to be open and trust me.

I wasn't kidding in the least bit when I told her how I feel. If anything, it grows stronger with each passing day. It sucks I had to leave her right afterward, to head out on this run. The job has to get done, though, and my brothers will look after her. I'm hoping the time apart will give us each a chance to think on things without the other being right there to influence our feelings. So far, however, the distance has only made me want her more. I keep looking to the future, and she's always included in those thoughts.

"Seems too good to be true," Angel snarls, keeping his voice quiet. He's my backup, along with his prospect, Lunatic. The club wasn't too keen on me doing the job myself. The only way I got them all to agree to the vote for it was with the club enforcer having my back. Along with his twisted project Lunatic, to take the fall in case we got caught. Luna doesn't know that last little bit of the plan though, as I'm sure he wouldn't exactly volunteer himself to get locked up on the account of us. I'm more than capable of snuffing this rich fucker out, but the club doesn't want me, their prez, risking my neck.

Bastard

My brothers don't realize that I have to be the one to do this. I'm keeping good on my word. While Alice may not know a fuckin' thing about what I'm doing out here to keep her at my club, she's not completely oblivious. She's smart enough to see that something big is going down, and to know it's gotta be significant if her pops has agreed to letting her stay with me at the compound so far.

I told the senator I'd do what I had to-to take care of his request, and I meant it. Powerhouse and Whiskey have taken to Alice, so they've agreed to keep a close watch on her while I'm out of state. The last thing I need to be concerned about while on a job is her safety and well-being. If that so-called threat the senator had previously mentioned decides to show up, I'm going to lose my shit and hightail it back home to fuck somebody up. At least with me killing this john, the senator will know I'm dead fucking serious about burying anyone who thinks they can fuck with Alice—in any aspect. I won't play with her life. As far as I'm concerned, her father is as much a threat to her as anyone.

I cast an impatient glance at Angel and crack my neck. It's time to handle this shit and get the fuck outta here. I have a woman waiting on me and that's the best sort of motivation to hurry the fuck up and take care of business.

The huge fucker nods to me and orders Lunatic to stay behind as our lookout. The stubborn enforcer pushes inside through the back door. It's one of those doors filled with windowpanes you can easily kick in. I guess the owner didn't think about security with the back entry either, since it leads out to a sparkling heated sapphire pool.

The brothers and I each hold our own set of talents—aside from killing, anyhow. For example, Angel isn't only responsible for death, but is also smooth as glass when it comes to breaking and entering. You wouldn't think that by his massive bulk. If you know anything about my brother, however, you'd be aware that he's the quiet type. That trait works like a charm for him slipping into places undetected.

I, on the other hand, am a jack of varied trades. I dabble in whatever the fuck heeds my attention. The upside of being prez is I can do whatever I want.

The door opens soundlessly. There's not even a creak to give away our position, thanks to the new construction. We slip inside, already aware of which side of the house our prey is on. The uppity motherfucker was stupid enough to leave all his lights off when he was gone. Once he stepped over the threshold, he was flipping on lights as he went. It was like a beacon, and our luck doubled in size when we realized his family didn't come home with him. That could've been a hiccup, as I won't stand for hurting innocent women and children, but no need to think on it now. I can put a few bullets in him, courtesy of my silencer and the world will be rid of one more perverted fucker with a God complex.

Our steps are nearly silent as we move together, careful not to bump into anything. I take the lead with Angel at my back. The brothers always got my six and that's a damn good feeling to have about a Royal Bastard.

His hand hits the middle of my back, and I reach behind me. He passes me his blade. I wasn't trying to get messy, I brought a silencer to make this quick and easy, but Angel's plan must've shifted. I wonder what he saw to make that call. Regardless, I trust him and his instinct. He's our enforcer because he knows what the fuck he's doing when it comes to this shit. I palm the blade handle, ready to make my move and step closer to the doorway that's cast in warm light.

The opportunity comes sooner than I'd anticipated when my mark opens the door. He steps into the dark hallway and I hold my breath. His eyes widen comically as he finally notices us and I'm suspended in the moment, my head suddenly blank on what to do.

Angel leaps past me like a limber fucking panther. He grabs the guy with such force he doesn't have a chance to react. My brother spins the john toward me, and rather than a quick slice across the throat, I go for his meaty gut. With Angel holding him securely, I plunge the knife into his stomach again and again. Blood gurgles out the man's mouth, mimicking the holes I've poked in his middle.

The dark crimson trails over his lips, to smear down his cleanly shaven chin. Angel steps backward, releasing the body to unceremoniously fall to the ground. He flops down like a dead fish and a chuckle makes its way free from me. I wasn't expecting that to happen just then, and I've got a case of the laughs.

Angel glares, shaking his head at me. The fucker's always serious, even at a time like this.

"Hey, don't look at me like that. You could've stuck him a couple times too, but you handed over your knife."

He complains, "I had a feeling something wasn't gonna go as planned."

"That explains why you changed things up. I was wondering."

He shrugs. "That and after seeing his daughter's photos on the wall, I figured we could torch the place."

"Burn it all?" I probe, staring at him like he's lost his mind. With Angel, he probably has.

"Yeah, erase everything about this scum. They'll get the insurance money along with a fresh start."

"Ah." I nod, understanding where he's going with this. "Bet. Let's fuckin' do it then, brother."

"You go out the back. I get to torch this place, since you had all the other fun," he declares dejectedly.

I flash a quick, amused grin, thoroughly enjoying his grumpiness at me getting in the kill and not him. Wiping the blade on my black jeans, I pass his knife over. "All right, then, sour puss. Take care of it, and I'll catch you in a beat. I'll go make sure your prospect hasn't fucked anything up."

Angel puts his knife away, his irises sparkling with malevolence. I guess setting a huge mansion on fire elicits some kind of emotion out of the crazy fucker. Now that this guy's out of my way, I have one more person in line to take care of. Once my club figures out who the fuck has been threatening my woman, then it's hell to pay. I'll be able to relax again once I put their body in the ground and know my woman's safely by my side.

I wait in the backyard, in the shadows with Lunatic for Angel to come out. We're next to the sparkling sapphire pool, chlorine and moisture permeates the air stealing away some of the allure it holds at first sight. It takes my brother all of about three minutes to make it out the back door. He's looking much more relaxed now as well.

"All set?" I ask, although I already know his answer.

"Mm," he confirms, sending me a nod. "Let's get the fuck outta here, Prez. This place will be going up in bright flames any minute now, and we don't need to be around when it happens. Come on, Luna, you got our flank."

"Gotcha, brother," I mutter. "The light wouldn't be a good thing in a home invasion," I let a twisted chuckle escape.

We hightail it down the road to where we've parked our rental van. We rode our motorcycles up here, of course, but rented the nondescript cage for this particular job when we got into the city. In a rich neighborhood like this, someone's always getting shit updated or fixed, so no one thinks twice about a white van being parked on the side of the road. Fucking idiots, they should realize it's burglary 101 when it comes to criminals to have a plain vehicle like this. Still, they couldn't be fucked to pay attention. They'd damn sure call the cops if my loud ass pipes went ripping through their neighborhood though.

We head for the hotel, ready to get cleaned up and call it a night. Angel and Lunatic can do whatever the fuck they want tonight, but I'll be passing the hell out. I plan to be up early to hit the road, I want to be back at the club as soon as possible. We're risking our necks up here in another MC's territory, as well as the gangs this shit hole seems to breed, let alone for committing murder and arson.

"I'm guessing it went well, since you didn't die." Blow greets me in the parking lot as we pull our bikes to a stop in front of the club.

I release a snort. "Missed you, too, motherfucker. Glad to hear you were worried about us."

He grins at my response and nods to Angel, ignoring the grumpy prospect in the back who rode behind us the entire way. The brother and his minion must've drunk all night when we got to the hotel as they were hungover as fuck for the whole ride home.

"How's things?" I ask, heading for the door.

"Fine. Most of us have sold our stashes already, so we're gonna need to go on another run soon and pick up some powder."

"Good. When we're selling, we're making money."

"I may've snorted a chunk of my brick, but you can take it outta my cut."

I shake my head. He's been escaping reality more and more lately, it seems. I wonder if this has anything to do with Maddy's absence? "Don't let it get outta hand. You're still the motherfuckin' VP of this club, brother."

"I know, I know. I like to party, what can I say?"

I gripe, "You can pull your big boy panties on. We'll discuss this further in church."

"When you callin' it, so I can let the brothers know?"

"Later. I want to see Alice for a bit, then I'll update everyone on what all went down."

"Bet." He veers off as I head through the club in search of my woman. She's been on my mind constantly since I took off, and I can't wait to see her gorgeous ass.

"Gem?" I call as I cross the threshold to my room. It's nothing special, just your standard bedroom with a small bathroom. There's barely room in there for a shower, but I get by with it just fine. I could've demanded more space, being prez, but I refuse to take away any extra from my brothers.

"Hm?" She rolls over, parting those pretty irises of hers.

"Babe, you're actually taking a nap?"

Alice sits up, sleepily rubbing her hands over her face. She sends me a half-awake smile that has my world tilting on its axis. She's absolutely stunning like this, all mussed up, waiting for me in the middle of my bed. "I didn't sleep well the past few days with you gone," she admits. It shouldn't make me feel good inside, but I'm a selfish asshole, and it does.

"Did dickless end up taking you swimming?" I ask on a possessive growl. I've grown a bit selfish over my woman in the time she's come to stay here. She makes me happy, so I seem to try and drown myself in her any chance I get.

She flashes me an amused grin. "As much as I begged, Richardson still didn't relent. So, you can relax, tough guy."

"You can beg me for something," I rasp, desire coating my voice. I crawl toward her, starting from the foot of the bed. She opens her arms, welcoming me and I fall into her warmth. She feels so fucking good wrapped around me that I can't help but groan in comfort.

"What is it?" she asks on a near whisper.

"I like the way you feel, I like seeing you in my bed, and I like you."

She giggles. "Well, that's a relief. I couldn't tell by the dickin' you gave me before you left."

I chuckle. "I can't believe you just said *dickin'*, babe. I'm pulling you over to the dark side."

"You're corrupting me."

"And I'm not sorry for it, one bit," I admit, tucking my face into her neck to rain my assault of kisses over her flesh. It makes her squirm and my heart beats so fast I feel like it may never stop. I pull her hand from under me and place it against my chest. "You feel that, Gem?"

"Your heartbeat?"

"Yep, it's going fast for you. It only does that when you're close to me."

"Aww, that's the sweetest thing you've ever said to me!" The skin around her eyes crinkles from her smiling so widely in return.

"Nah, pretty sure that was when I told you that you have a bomb pussy."

"Uh," she groans, rolling her eyes and I can't help but grin like a lovesick fool. "I'm glad you're home. I missed you."

"Home," I repeat.

"Oh, yeah?"

"I just realized that's what you are to me. I always thought it was the MC, but it's you. Gem, you feel like home, all warm and welcoming, and mine. There's no other place I'd rather be." When I glance at her face again, she's got tears in her eyes. Happy ones, I hope. I lean in, pressing my mouth to hers. I suck the sweet flesh between my lips, making her open for me. My tongue dives inside, reuniting with hers.

Alice moves underneath me. I realize she's shoving the bedding down off her and my hands come in contact with her smooth, bare skin.

"Fuck!" I draw away enough to allow the curse to escape. "You're naked, aren't you?" I flick my gaze downward, discovering her body on display, ready for me. "Jesus, Gem, you're trying to kill me, aren't you?"

She giggles again, and it's the sweetest sound—like pure honey. My woman is happy. What more can a man ask for? I yank my wrinkled old shirt over my head, not giving a shit that I have road grime on me still. We can take a shower together after this, and I'll worship her body all over again. I manage to kick off my boots, sending them flying from the bed, then I'm moving to force my jeans down off my hips. I don't wear underwear; it's just a waste of time, in my opinion. Besides, I like having the freedom to whip my cock out whenever I need to. With Alice, that seems to be frequently, as I can't get my fill of her sexy ass.

Grasping my hard cock, I rub the tip through her wet center. Her core's ready and waiting for me to thrust inside. I hope she greets me this way after every run I go on. "You want my cock?"

"Yes, Ripper. I've been waiting ever since you left."

"Damn, you sure do know how to make a man feel special."

"I try." She flashes me a flirty smile.

Thrusting my hips forward, I slide home. She's tight and needy, just the way I enjoy the most. If I had to stay in bed with this woman for the rest of my life, I'd die a lucky man. That thought is crazy considering how quickly things have progressed between us, but it's the truth. My pops always told me that if I find something that makes me feel good and it isn't illegal or will kill me, then to keep doing it. At the time, he was speaking about our motorcycles, but it fits here, too. Alice is exactly the type of respite I need to have in my life. She's a damn fine woman, with one hell of a smart head on her shoulders. I couldn't ask for anymore when it comes to the right ol' lady to have at my side.

"Goddamn, your pussy feels good. Not gonna lie, Gem, I don't think I'll ever get my fill of it or you."

"Those words are starting to sound like forever. I thought that sort of thing was supposed to scare bad boys off," she finishes with a groan as I swivel my hips, raking my groin across her clit.

"Boys, maybe, but I'm a motherfuckin' man."

"Yes, you are, indeed. A very big, sexy, stubborn man."

I trail my tongue down her throat, over her shoulders and the tender, creamy skin of her breasts. "But I'm yours," I mutter in my pursuit, making her hum in delight.

She pushes her chest upward, wanting my mouth on her stiff nipples. They're deliciously marked up from our wild fucking before I took off on the road. I had to leave her something to think of me by, and each time she looked in the mirror, she'd see me all over her body. I'm not usually the chest beating, leashing type of brother when it comes to my woman, but I'll be damned if I don't mark her as mine in some sort of way. It's an honor, after all, to be able to call her all mine.

"I'm a bastard, baby, that pretty much describes me to a T," I mutter cockily, making her snicker some more. "Fuck, I love hearing you giggle. Sweetest thing I've heard all day."

Her hands shove against my chest and I take the hint, rolling us over until she's on top. I've picked up on her sexual habits, and I don't mind having her rock that perfect ass on me. She rides me, tilting her hips leisurely while staring down at me with lust filled irises. She knows this drives me mad inside with desire for her. She's the sexiest fucking woman, especially when she's all prim and properly buttoned up in her casual suit attire. She wears that shit around the club all the time, her skirts and those special shirts you call a blouse. Jesus, she has me lifting her knee length skirts up her thighs and untucking those blouses at least twice a day to attempt to get my fill with her.

Her hair falls forward, the locks tickling my abs, making them clench up. "You're so handsome," she whispers, running her nails over my flexed abs. She twists my nipples, copying my movements, making my eyes roll back.

"Faster, Gem. Fuck, the pressure is building too much."

"Good, I want you to feel the same thing you do to me."

"Yeah? I make you wanna combust when I'm driving my fat cock inside you?"

She nods.

"Say it. I wanna hear the words leave your proper, pouty little mouth, baby."

"Oh," she moans, her head falling back as she gets closer to her orgasm. The new position pushes her breasts outward again, and I reach up, covering the ample globes with my palms. She's more than a handful, the perfect amount to slip my dick between and fuck. "I love when your cock's inside me, Ripper. You make me go wild with wanting to come all over it."

"Fuck, yes!" I growl in approval, dropping my hands to her waist to hold her as I drive my hips upward.

"Oh!" she screams. "Ripper! God!"

It's my undoing, and I charge over the ledge of restraint. My cock throbs, my orgasm taking over to drown out my thoughts with a blinding light mixed with intense pleasure. With each powerful pulse of my cock, my cum shoots deep inside her I gave up attempting condoms with her. She was making me come so much that I was breaking right through the fucking things. I took it as a sign that I'm meant to be inside her, meant to fill her with my seed.

"Goddamn, Alice," I huskily rasp, reaching up to place my palms on her cheeks. I lean up, pulling her to me so I can kiss her again. "I swear it gets better each time."

"I know...I feel it too," she confirms, eagerly meeting my kiss, mating our tongues. She's making this so easy and yet so fucking hard for me all at once. I could love this woman—hell, I already do. There's no denying it. If something were to happen and I lost her, I don't know what I'd do. Lord knows I'm starting to see that I don't want to live my life without her in it. Like they say on those jewelry commercials...a diamond is forever, and she's mine.

Chapter 15

"It's impossible," said pride. "It's risky,"
said experience. "It's pointless," said reason.
"Give it a try," whispered the heart.
- Unknown

Church

"It's good to have you guys back," Whiskey rumbles at the table toward Angel and me, and the brothers jump in to agree. He sits back in his chair, rubbing his belly. There's not much there, but the distinguished fucker acts like he's a fat bastard or something.

This is the first full church session that Wrench is sitting in on, and I know he's going to bring up the idea of Alice's bodyguard prospecting. I'm not sure what I think of it, to be honest. Richardson's got a hefty set of nuts for standing up for my woman, especially when it comes to me. If he's caught some feelings for her, however, I'm not sure I can handle having him in my club and not end up slitting his throat at the first wrong move he makes.

"Thanks." I accept Whiskey's greeting, along with the other brothers. "Let's also welcome in Wrench. He's a fully-patched member at our table now. Guess at some point, we need to set up a celebration for the newest Royal Bastard, aye?" The brothers around him pat him on the back and everyone else reaches in to pound his fist. "You earned it, Wrench. You've sacrificed for the club, and we've come to trust you, to think of you as our brother."

"'Preciate that, Prez." Wrench smirks, pulling his solid black ball cap a bit lower, not used to having everyone's attention on him at once. He's got the typical mechanic look. You know the type, tan from working outside on vehicles and always has a bit of grease on him somewhere, especially on his faded jeans. He's got eyes the color of Jack Daniels with short, inky hair and a light smattering of scruff on his face to match. I'd like to think he fits in pretty well around here and will more so now that he's got his Royal Bastards and one percenter patches adorning his leather vest.

"I know you want to bring something to the table."

He nods, moving to rest his hands on the solid wood in front of him. He cracks his knuckles, watching me. They're bloodied up; I'd suspect from him banging them on parts while fixing shit. Lord knows it happens to the best of us.

It's been many years since I got patched in, yet I can still remember the feeling of sitting at the table for the first time. It's a respected and coveted place in the club, and that shit can be intimidating as fuck. Church is sacred, so no one would've told a prospect jack about what goes on and what to expect. I'm sure Wrench had his own theories, but who knows if it was anything like this.

Plague lights up a blunt, inhaling deeply before passing it over to our new brother. He must be able to read the nervousness in the other man like I can. Coming from Plague, that weed will no doubt be laced and fuck the brothers up fairly quickly. Wrench gratefully accepts the Mary Jane, taking a few quick puffs before passing it along to the next brother. I'm sure he wants to hold on to it and smoke it down, but in our club, we share. It's puff, puff, pass, or else you get a fist to the gut for being a stingy motherfucker.

"We discuss any of that sort at the end of church," I inform him, not wanting to leave him hanging out to dry on the way things work around here.

"Sounds good," he says. His eyes are already beginning to glaze over with the drug's effects. We'll get some business handled, and our new brother will end up stoned out of his mind.

"First up, our trip was successful. Me and Angel didn't hit any snags. We were beginning to believe that shit went a little too easily. Something always seems to fuck up, no matter how small it may be."

Plague speaks up. "I haven't heard anything. I've kept my eyes and ears to the ground for any suspicious reports since you left to around the time you two were up there. So far, there's been a police and fire report filed. The paperwork was on a house fire in an uppity neighborhood, and ol' Senator Compton's opposition dying a tragic death. They haven't opened up about much to the media, but from what I've gathered, they have no leads."

Blow whoops. "That's some damn good news! Love easy paydays." He's always hyped up from his coke habit, not that I mind. I'm used to it, and as long as he takes care of his club business, then I won't intervene.

Angel complains, "Easy for you, maybe. I just had to ride up into the fucking bullshit cold weather. My dick was shriveled up for three motherfuckin' days."

Powerhouse chuckles, amused with Angel's harping. The brother rarely bitches, so when he does, we tend to take notice. Powerhouse is the only one crazy enough to rip on Angel about it, too, as Angel's a mean motherfucker. He won't hesitate to break your nose if you piss him off enough.

I nod, agreeing with my enforcer. We're far too used to being spoiled by mild winters and warm springs in Texas that one ride up north, that's not in the summer, had my asshole clenching too. "He's not lying, I fuckin' froze too. No wonder those people up there are so bitter. I'd be pissed off if I had to live in that shit too."

The brothers chuckle.

I pull my phone out, showing the device to everyone. "I'm putting the call through to the senator." Each member quiets, waiting. I hit Senator Compton's icon and put the call on speaker for them to hear as well. This is club business, so they have every right to listen in on my call.

"Senator Compton." Alice's crooked father answers immediately. He picks up right away since it's business, but if I had to guess, he hasn't taken Alice's calls since he left. She admitted to me how he's been manipulating her and that this is one way he likes to try and guilt trip her. I guess he's done that sorta bullshit in the past with the women in his life. He's a fucking pussy using manipulation to control them.

"Royal Bastards here," I inform him curtly, scowling at my phone, not that he can see me or anything. "Wanted to put in a call and let you know that my promise has been kept."

"That's good news." The relief in his voice is beyond evident and has me rolling my eyes. He's a dumbass if he thought I couldn't pull the hit off. We do that shit any time it's necessary.

"For you. Now, where is the club's good news? When's Baker getting released?"

"It's in progress, I assure you. It may take a few more weeks, but I'm not expecting it to."

"For your sake, I sure as fuck hope not." My brothers grunt and nod their agreements with me. We all want Baker back. He's family.

"And my daughter?" he mentions. I can't help but rumble with a possessive growl at him bringing her up.

"Is being well taken care of," I bark impatiently. "Don't jeopardize it by screwing us over. If you want a health and wellness check on Alice, I suggest you call her yourself. Ask for a goddamn selfie or something."

"Noted. Thank you for handling my problem. I'll have my man Jenkins reach out to you when we have a release date and further details. I'm glad we could form this little relationship. I may need your help in the future."

"As long as Alice is here, then I'll take your calls. You mess with her, and things will change very quickly. She's the only reason why we have this arrangement, you feel me?"

He ignores my last statement. "She doesn't want to come home yet?" the entitled fucker asks, shock coating his words.

"Nope. In fact, I think she wants to become a Texan. Maybe permanently."

He scoffs, but is smart enough to keep his comments to himself. "Business calls, I'll be in touch soon."

I hang up and glance around the table, landing on Angel. "Send a persuasive note informing the good senator that his daughter will only be safe if she remains at the club. I don't want him to try and pull any sly shit now that he has what he wants. He needs to believe that whoever is after her will only back off if she's under Royal Bastard's protection. I want an extra ace up my sleeve in case he decides he wants both of his daughters."

I rake my hands through my hair, feeling the semi-stiff texture from my gel and exhale, knowing I just fucked my hairstyle up. My woman was determined to tame it before church and I let her, liking the way her hands felt on me far too much to tell her no. Hell, I would've let her do anything as long as she'd kept touching me.

I continue speaking, reasoning, "Maybe if he believes Alice is in more danger at home, he'll back the fuck off on making her return. She's freaked out enough that he's going to come for her, and I won't have that shit anymore. He ever shows up unannounced, you shoot first and bury him out past the airport. My woman doesn't need to have him dragging her down any longer." And I'm dead fucking serious. I'd do it myself, but I can't have her hating me for it if she were to ever catch wind of it. It sounds fucked up, but I've never been a saint. I'm an outlaw.

"Consider it done," Angel concurs without hesitation. "They'll never know where the letter came from, only that the consequences are severe if not followed to a T. As for the suit, you say the word and it'll be handled."

I nod toward him with gratitude. "Appreciate it."

Whiskey leans in, and I cast my gaze at our treasurer. "Now that it's over with and you kept up your side of the bargain to her father, you making Alice your ol' lady? *Officially*, I mean?"

I scrub my hand over my face, then fold my arms over my chest. These are serious conversations we're having today, and to be honest, I wasn't expecting to be digging this deep today. I'm caught off guard with it and the table's calling for my attention, wanting answers I need to give. I stare down at the wood grain, not sure what the right thing to say is. I exhale, blowing out a breath as Blow jumps in to offer his two cents, obviously picking up on my indecision.

"You made that deal thinking of her, Prez. I'm not getting sappy or anything, for fuck's sake, but I've never seen you this up around a bitch before. I've watched you get your cock sucked by countless women, and none of them have had you smiling and parading them around the clubhouse like they're your queen bee. You damn near growl and rip out anyone's throat who so much as looks in her direction. Not used to you bein' such a possessive fucker."

"My *queen...*" I mutter, more to myself than my brothers. "I like that."

Powerhouse agrees. "He's right, Prez. We all like her. She's a good woman, especially for you and the club. If you want to know what any of us think, to make the decision easier on you, maybe you should ask." He's my SAA, the club's previous enforcer, and he's consistently honest with me. It's one of the things I've always respected about him—that, and his fierce sense of loyalty to the Royal Bastards. This club is as much of his life, as it is mine.

"Don't get me wrong, I want her. Fuck, I want to keep her so badly, I just don't know if this life would be good for her. It's easy for me to put my patch on her and stick her on the back of my bike...but is it really fair for her to have to give up everything she knows? We come from two opposite ends of the spectrum, and I won't lie, I'm falling for her pretty fucking hard and fast. When you care for someone like that, you're supposed to do what's best for them, not what you want." There're a few grunts of agreement, making me glance around and ask the rest of them, "You've got opinions?"

"Whiskey snorts. "You know damn well we do, jackass."

"Then give 'em to me."

He begins. "She's a real sweetheart. She's genuine and has a good heart. I'm all for you making her permanent around here, but she's the type of woman that deserves a one-woman man. If you're willing to give up outside pussy, then stop overthinking it."

Angel speaks up next. "I don't know her, but I want you to be happy. If she makes you that way, then put her on the back of your bike. You're already trying to make her life easier and shit, thinking of ways to be a better man for her."

Wrench goes next. "She's the only female around this place to ever make me a sandwich and bring it to the garage while I was in there working all day. She thinks of others—not just herself, and around here, that's a must. She's already a sister to me." He shrugs and I can't help but grin at his description. He's completely right. Alice is one of the most selfless people I've ever met.

Plague carries on. "I don't mind her a bit, and she stays out of the way of club shit. She was freaked out by the strippers at first, but she apologized and rolled on. She could treat the other girls around here like shit, being that she's a lady and all, but she doesn't. If you're gonna have a woman, being the prez, she's the type of bitch you need by your side."

Blow finishes up. "I'm with them. You made a serious deal because of her. You took care of that shit yourself, all while checking back on her here to make sure she's straight. I really don't see why this is even a discussion for you. We gave you our blessing when we voted on the senator's deal. We've already agreed to protect her. It's done, as far as I'm concerned."

I nod. "You're my brothers. My family. This isn't only my club, but all of ours. I respect each of you, that's why I've taken this into consideration so much. Not only that, but I want her to be content too. It's been fucking my head up, wondering if this is the smartest move. You're right, though, I love that woman, and it's past time I let her know as much."

My brothers grin and cheer. I only hope that when their time comes around and they fall for a bitch, that I can be just as supportive. Ol' ladies are sacred to this club. It's something we agreed on from day one, and it looks like I'll be the first of us to bring one into the fold. If there's anyone that can handle the pressure though, it's Alice. My woman is so fuckin' strong and smart, she makes me damn proud to have her by my side.

"All right, all right, moving on from my personal life. Now that we're talking about Alice, though, has anyone found any information about who wants to hurt her? We've got plenty of shady ass contacts. I'm hoping someone pulled through with some intel."

The brothers grumble and curse, complaining they don't have any leads. Except Angel. He says, "I may have something…I don't know what yet. I have a few people that're supposed to be getting back to me. I'll let you know as soon as I hear from them, whether it's something or nothing."

"Fuck, I hope they know who it is. If you find them, Angel, I want them to fucking pay!" I demand viciously. "Everyone else keep trying as well. This is my top priority right now, aside from the senator's bullshit and our regularly scheduled drug runs. Now, anybody else have something to discuss?"

Wrench gestures, and I nod to him. He mutters, the weed taking over. His eyes are red and glazed over, and he has a persistent smirk that he can't seem to drop right now. "I understand that part of being a patched member is nominating a prospect."

Blow confirms, "It's not a requirement, but our charter prefers to include it. It's a way to make us stronger and have loyalty surround us, versus random fuckers just showin' up. Don't feel pressured right away, unless you have someone in mind already."

"I do. I've been speaking to Mark over these past few weeks and he's shown interest. He'll also want to stick around if Prez's ol' lady stays in Texas."

Whiskey stares at him quizzically and huffs, "Who the fuck is Mark?"

Wrench drops the smirk, his lips turning downward. "It's Alice's bodyguard. You know, she calls him Richardson?"

Powerhouse and Blow break out into laughs. Plague asks, "His name is Mark? That's so fucking plain. I though his name was Richardson and he pissed off his momma when he was born or something and she punished him by giving him that long ass first name. Seemed a fitting curse to me." He shrugs.

We all shake with laughter.

"Fine, we can vote on it, but Wrench?" He stares at me intently, taking in my stern glare. "If he has feelings for my woman, it'll be hell to pay. I may make you take him out to bum fuck Egypt and shoot his ass just because you nominated him. You can dig the motherfuckin' hole out past the airport for his body, too. You feel me?"

"Got it, Prez."

"Good. All in favor of allowing Marky-Mark-the-cursed to prospect, say aye." We vote unanimously, and it's quickly settled. "You remember how Whiskey showed you the ropes when you came around?" I question Wrench. He's starting to come back around, his high already wearing off. He must be having anxiety like a motherfucker. Plague's blunts will keep you toasted for hours if you're calm, but this dumbass is burning through it like he's immune or something.

"Yeah, he was cool with me, even though I was green. Everyone else treated me like shit." He shakes his head and the brothers laugh. It wasn't him specifically. All the prospects have to go through a rough time to earn our loyalty and respect. We each did it, too, so it's fair.

"Right. Well, it's now your responsibility to do the same for him. Show him the ropes, but also keep in mind that he's Alice's security. He can shoot the shit and do grunt work when he's not busy keeping my woman safe."

"I can do that, no problem."

"I'm counting on it. You have any questions, you hit up Blow. That new fucking prospect needs to keep his distance with me until I'm certain he doesn't have a thing for my ol' lady."

"I'll make sure he stays in line and let him know what's expected of him," Wrench confirms.

I nod. "And that shit he pulled before I left, standing up to me in the bar? You may want to clue him in, that sort of bullshit will get his ass beat. I admire him being loyal to my woman and all, but when it comes to joining the club, that loyalty has to shift to *me* and the Royal Bastards."

He nods, and I check around the table for anything else. No one speaks up, so I call an end to church.

Now that the business side is taken care of, I need to speak to Alice. The sooner we can figure everything out, the better. I can't wait to see her gorgeous flesh wrapped in my colors, letting the whole world know she's mine. *My ol' lady.*

Chapter 16

> He alone is my rock and my salvation,
> my fortress where I will not be shaken.
> - Psalm 62:6

Alice

"You sure did get lucky hooking the Prez," Cindy says dreamily, sounding a bit more from the East Coast than Texas. She stares at the wall with their mugshots, making heart eyes at all of the Royal Bastards members. I can't help but smile. It's ridiculous that we're looking at their mugshots and fantasizing about the guys. I've only got one particular brother on my mind, but still, never in a million years did I think I'd ever be doing this at some point in my life.

"You think I've hooked him?" I ask, turning to look at her. She blows kisses at each photo, making me giggle. She may be a sweetbutt around here, a term I'm not fond of, but she doesn't act like some of the slutty girls did that I've met before. They were always so vicious, like female vipers with boobs. Cindy's more of a sweetheart than a sweetbutt, in my opinion.

She flashes me a wide smile. "Oh, girl, you definitely did. That man has it bad for you. He's never asked me to sneak out with him in the past to help him meet up with another woman. Once he told me about you, I knew you had to be someone real special. Prez is a decent man. He may be rough around the edges and all, but he takes care of everyone here. Gotta have a big heart to take on so much responsibility, if you ask me."

I grin, concurring with her. "I completely agree with you, Cindy. I also wanted to thank you. You've been nice to me from the moment I got here. You could've been rude, but you chose to make me feel welcome instead."

"I don't think you realize what it means to be with the prez, doll. What he says is the law around here, and he's treating you like his woman. It may not mean much to you, but 'round here, that's a huge deal. Take that new seat he got put on his motorcycle for example. He did that so you'd have a place and be comfortable. In this world, it's like him buying a ring for you and showing the entire club."

My mouth pops open with a gasp. "You can't be serious."

She beams, enjoying the attention. "Oh, I am, and apparently Prez is too."

I can't help but laugh at her excitement over it all.

"Well, it certainly makes it more fun to have you enthusiastic about it for me."

"It means he'll take an ol' lady. That's big babe, real big. Just please, don't kick me out, I promise to leave your man alone."

"I would never kick you out! Besides, it's not my place to."

She snorts. "Thank God, you're such a good woman, Alice. You're gaining so much influential power toward the club, and you don't even realize it. The prez may be in charge, but when a man like that finds his golden pussy, then she's the one with the true power."

"I don't understand."

"Honey, a man like Ripper would do anything for his ol' lady, for his golden pussy. All you'd have to do is ask, and he'd burn the whole world down for you."

We're interrupted by the door to church swinging open, and the club members pouring out.

"You eavesdroppin'?" Angel practically growls, vibrating with hostility at Cindy.

She pales. "N-no, I was just talking with Alice, honest, and making sure the mugshots didn't need cleaning."

The broody enforcer grunts, snagging her wrist in his big paw. He tugs her along behind him and she manages to get a quick wave off to me. I return it, a bit worried. I hope he doesn't take it out on her, thinking she was trying to listen to their church session. Ripper explained it to me that it's a private room they meet in to discuss club business. He said it's for patched members only and considered a sacred spot for the Royal Bastards. Being around my father so much, I understand completely about secret meetings and what not. I've also learned it's best to keep my nose out of it. In some cases, the less you know, the better.

Whiskey offers me a flirty wink and a grin that says he knows far too much about my relationship with Ripper. I am, however, glad to have the older man's approval as I can tell he means a great deal to the man in question. I offer Whiskey a wave and a kind smile in return.

Blow's next to come out of the private room, but he ignores me completely. I'm not sure if he doesn't like me, or if it has to do with my sister. Regardless, I wish I knew how to make it better. Ripper told me about Blow and Madison spending a lot of time together, and it's only made me feel increasingly guilty for leading my father to her.

Powerhouse beams his big, friendly smile as he passes. "Dollface." He nods and I offer him the same smile I shared with Whiskey. The massive beast of a man is like a giant teddy bear when it comes to women. He's seriously the sweetest guy around this place, and he's always helping someone out.

Plague and Wrench come strolling out together, speaking quietly about a new prospect they plan to whip into shape. They're too engrossed to pay much attention to me standing around—awkwardly, now that I'm alone. Wrench manages a muttered, "Ma'am," and I blush at his formality.

I anxiously wait for my favorite biker, but he doesn't leave the room. I take in the men behind me. They're at the bar grabbing drinks. They chitchat, but none of them mention their prez, and it has my curiosity growing by the moment.

I take a few steps in the direction of the sacred room. Above the door is a wooden sign that's been carved and stained a deep walnut color. It says Royal Bastards Church, No Excuses. I have no idea what it implies, but one thing is clear, I'm not welcome inside. I stand in the open doorway and knock on the wall. I'm not brave enough to cross the threshold without an invitation. I have too much respect for Ripper and his brothers. This is their home; I'm merely a guest.

He glances up, brow wrinkled until he notices it's me. He flashes me his signature cocky grin.

"Hey, baby," I greet huskily and he stands.

He quickly strides to me, pushing me a step backward away from church to wrap me in his arms. "Gem," he breathes my name like it's a prayer. He closes the door behind him, leaving behind any thoughts he was thinking over in there.

"I was, uh, waiting for you," I admit, a bit embarrassed over it. "But got worried when you never left the room."

"You don't need to fret over me, Gem. That's my job, remember?"

"How's it fair if you can worry over me and protect me, but I can't do the same?" I ask. "You can't carry the weight of the club and everyone in it on your shoulders alone."

"You'd protect me?" he asks, cocking his head to the side. *He's so damn cute, all rough and tough and messy.*

"Of course, I would. We've talked about us meaning a lot to each other, and I was serious Ripper. I-I don't want to scare you off, but I think I'm falling in love with you. It scares me. I don't think it should be happening like this and so soon, but I just can't stop thinking about you. Even when you're right here, just in the other room, I need to know you're okay, that you're safe and happy. I want to help you with this burden, even if you don't see it as one."

"Christ, woman," he murmurs against my hair, pulling me close. "It's like you're speaking from my own heart. I'm not used to being mushy like this, but when it comes to you, I don't even mind it. In fact, you're always on my mind too. Truth is, I don't think I could stop worrying or thinking or wanting you if I tried to fight it. I'm in too fuckin' deep."

I tilt my head against his shoulder so I can press a kiss to his scruffy, sharp jawline. He's got the sort of chin that I'd bet men get broken hands hitting. He's hard all over, yet surprisingly soft when he's got me in his arms. I lean in, kissing his jaw again, wanting to have more of him. He's too tall for me to kiss his cheek like this unless I reach up on my tippy-toes.

"We need to have a chat, yeah?" he grumbles, tucking me under his arm and leading me away from church. Warning bells silently sound in my head.

Did I finally scare him off, and he's ready to cut me loose after all? He told me he wanted me, to be with him in the future and I believed him, but maybe I shouldn't have? By him being in too deep, does that mean he's getting rid of me before it has a chance to go any further? I have to be overreacting after what he just professed moments ago.

He leads me to his office, taking the seat behind his desk. He props me up against the solid wood, with my thighs between his legs. He sits back, his hands resting on the outsides of my knees. He glances up at me, soft sweetness reflecting in his irises. "You're so damn flawless, Gem. You're my diamond."

Blush steals over my cheeks. He ties me up in knots inside. "Thank you."

"I spoke to your father."

That's the last thing I was expecting to come out of his mouth. When he said he wanted to talk, I was foolish enough to believe he meant about him and me, not about my father's overbearing habits. "Oh, is he okay? Is everything all right?"

He nods. "Told 'im I wasn't ready to let you go, that I want you to stay here with me permanently."

I gasp, taken back that he was being serious before, when we'd spoken about a possible long-term picture. I can't believe he's actually spoken to my father on it. "What did he have to say about that?" *I'm sure he was enraged.* Only on the inside, though—my father never lets himself show anger as you never know when someone may be watching. He's always thinking of his campaign, twenty-four-seven.

Ripper shrugs, briefly squeezing my thighs, then moves to lightly rub circles into them again. "I assured him that you're being taken care of here and kept safe. I also reminded him of our budding friendship and he was able to see reason within it all."

"Just like that? He's never been so agreeable with anyone, when it comes to Madison or me. I don't understand."

"There's nothing *to* understand, babe. If you want to be with me, then you can be. You will."

"I-I do want that," I admit honestly, baring my true feelings to him. Damn the consequences, he needs to realize this isn't just a quick fling of sorts with me.

He stands, his tall body towering over me. He leans in to press his lips to mine, murmuring, "I want to claim you. I want you to be my ol' lady."

I moan against his lips. His serious, gravelly voice sounds so sexy, saying those things to me. "And you'll be my man?" I can't help but ask, to hope.

"I'll be your *ol' man*. In club life, that means we've chosen one another, for life. We're like penguins, babe. When we find the right woman, we're one and done."

I can't help but giggle. "You know you'll have to get a penguin tattoo now amidst all those skulls and what not you have decorating your skin."

He cracks a grin, the smug one that makes me fall a little harder for him each time he offers it up. "Gem, I'll get whatever tattoo you want me to. As long as you wear my patch, sayin' you're mine."

"A penguin with a diamond on her belly."

He wraps me tightly in his strong arms, making me feel safer than ever before. He releases a quiet chuckle, gazing at me, his hazel irises shining with so much emotion. "Anything, baby, just say you're my ol' lady. I need to fuckin' hear it."

"All right, *Prez*," I whisper huskily, running my hands over his firm pecs. "I'll be your ol' lady."

He pushes me backward onto the desk, spreading my legs apart. He shoves anything around us onto the floor, hovering his warm, heavy body over mine. He reminds me of a powerful beast, ready to mount his prey. "Keep callin' me prez, Alice. In fact, I wanna hear you fucking scream it. Every motherfucker in this place will know you've been claimed."

I can't help the wide smile I beam, as he throws my legs over his shoulders and dives in. He shoves my skirt up to my waist, gliding his hands over the inside of my thighs until he gets to my panties. He pushes them to the side, making room for his fingers and tongue. Ripper is insatiable when it comes to pleasing me, a fate I'm fortunate to have.

His tongue rains its delicious assault on me until I'm whimpering and my legs are shaking. One orgasm isn't enough, it seems. He's on a mission to make me have multiples. "Please!" I'm not above begging as my thighs quiver. He knows exactly how to touch me, whether it be with his tongue, his hands, or his cock. They all have me thanking God for bringing him into my life unexpectedly.

"Please, what?" he growls, his chest vibrating against my tender breasts.

"Please, Prez," I gasp as he sucks my clit wildly. My hands flail, clawing at whatever they come in contact with. "I-I want your cock inside me!" I shout. He's brought out my confidence when I'm with him like this, and he loves it when I tell him what I want him to do to me.

He pulls back to put enough space between us so he can unzip his jeans. He licks his lips that are shiny with my juices and pops his pants button. He gives them a shove off his hips and his cock springs out, ready to play. He leans in, dragging his tongue up the inside of my calf, humming in pleasure as he goes. The tip of his cock rests right at my entrance but he doesn't move to push inside anymore, the sensation driving me crazy. I want him to pound inside me so badly I could just scream and pound my fists. He told me to call him prez, and I did, but it didn't work like I'd hoped.

Ripper turns his head, licking up the inside of my other calf, making me squirm. His hips barely rock, just enough to tease my opening and let me feel the wetness on the tip of his cock. He wants me just as badly—the precum tells me as much. I lose my patience, huffing, "I want your cock, Prez. What do I have to do to get you to fuck me like you mean it?'

He responds with a growl, his lustful gaze meeting mine. "You want my cock?' His voice comes out gravelly and low. He's as turned on as I am, if not more.

"Yes. God, yes," I sigh.

He flashes me a wicked grin. "My cock is for my ol' lady," he taunts, and it's my breaking point.

I let out a frustrated scream. "I am your ol' lady, now fuck me!"

"Damn right, you are." He slams inside me so hard it brings tears to my eyes. "You better hold on, Gem, cause I'mma fuck this cunt so hard you never forget who the fuck you belong to, who your ol' man is." He pounds into me ruthlessly, repeatedly proclaiming I'm his property, that I'm his ol' lady, and if another man touches me that he'll kill them. It shouldn't turn me on so badly, but it does, and I come twice more. He waits until my third orgasm to finally spill himself inside me, and I've never felt so full—so cherished and warm.

Ripper scoops me up in his strong arms, holding me to his chest tenderly. He presses a kiss to my forehead and carries me out the door. "Gonna take you to our room. Gonna make love to my woman all fuckin' night," he grumbles like a selfish man and I can't help but love him for it. He makes me feel cherished, desired, and content. I can't help but pray I never have to give him up.

Epilogue

> Stay close to the people that make you feel like sunshine.
> - Unknown

Ripper

There's pounding on my door and I swear to fuck I'm gonna punch someone because of it. I was up all night long making love to my ol' lady. In the middle of it, she made us some food and we drank a few shots, then we went right back to drowning in each other. It was probably one of the best nights of my life, and that's no lie.

The pounding ensues, making Gem sleepily groan all cute and shit. Her curvy warm body snuggles into me even more. At this rate, she'll be working her way underneath me to get any closer. We held each other all night long when I wasn't inside her and that goes for when we finally passed out as well. I've never had a woman I've held so tightly before, not ever wanting to let her go. I still don't. It's too early for anyone to be bothering us.

"The fuck?" I shout, still keeping my eyes closed and my girl snug against me. "I'm gonna beat some ass!" I threaten only to hear Powerhouse chuckling on the other side of my door. I hear him speaking to someone, not giving a shit about being quiet, then there's loud rapping. It quickly morphs into pounding, along with Blow laughing his ass off loudly. *Stupid fucker.*

"Make it stop," Gem complains. I smirk to myself, giving her a quick squeeze and hop out of bed.

I jerk the door open, dick and all hanging on display for my brothers. They wanna bother me, then they'll get an eye full of cock. I cast a glare at the two of them and growl, "You want a motherfuckin' dentist appointment? Cause I'm about to knock your fucking teeth out," I threaten, willing to back up my words. I made Alice my ol' lady yesterday. That means we're in the honeymoon phase and deserve to be left alone for a bit.

They both burst into amused laughs, pissing me off further. Blow smacks Powerhouse on the shoulder, grinning like a fool at me. These two are trouble together, always into some sorta shit. Powerhouse says a little too cheerily, "Ma's here, she brought donuts."

My hand comes to my forehead, massaging my temples. *I didn't need this today.* I wanted some time to tell her about my woman before tossing Alice in her direction. With her showing up out of the blue on one of her little check-ins, I don't know how she'll react to my news. Sure, she was on my ass about me finding a woman, but I'm sure she has it in her head that she'll get a say in who that ol' lady ends up being. Ma knows her place, knows not to push her weight around with me, and that's the only reason why I'd consider her thoughts in the first place. I respect her and love her too much to hurt her. I hope this morning doesn't turn to shit after a damn good night. "Fuck."

Blow takes after Powerhouse's lead and says far too happily for my liking, "You got ten minutes, Prez. Or else, you know Ma will be coming in here. We'd enjoy seeing that, but thought we'd be nice and give your new ol' lady a heads up." The two fuckers snicker and turn tail, heading back in the opposite direction.

"Gem?"

"Mm," she responds, sprawled out, naked and face down. *Fuck, she's hot sprawled wide open for me. I could just climb right on the bed and slip my cock inside her like that. A good hard fuck is just what my body needs first thing—it's that or a gallon of coffee and no one speaking to me for thirty or so minutes. I'd take pussy over the coffee any day, start my morning out with a big fucking smile.* I'd do it too, crawl behind her and slip into that tight cunt, but I know she'll be far too sore today. I gotta take it easy on her till tomorrow, then she's fair game again. I'm not a completely heartless bastard, I love her swollen pink pussy too much to make it hate my cock already.

"Babe, we need to get up. My ma's here, and she's not usually the patient type. If we aren't out there soon, she'll come steam rolling in here."

Alice sits up, eyes wide, looking beautiful but also freaked the fuck out. "Ma...as in your mother?" she practically hisses, making me wince.

I nod, my balls shriveling a bit at my ol' lady's tone. I'm a hard bastard, but I love my woman and her scorn does not entice me unless I have the time to spank it out of her.

She squeals, glancing around the room in a panic. "Oh my God! I'm going to meet your mother and I know next to nothing about her! I'm so unprepared. Just look at me. I need a shower and make up and—"

I interrupt her. "I'm taking a shower really quick, and for the record, you're the most beautiful woman I've ever seen." I shrug with the small grain of truth and then walk my ass into my even smaller shower. In the next beat, I'm shoved into the corner as my woman comes flying into the space, shocking me that we can even fit in here together. She skips washing her hair, quickly covering her body in soap. She rubs up against me; I mean, it's impossible not to. She does pause long enough to shoot me this look, making me ask, "Yeah, babe?"

Her head tilts as she takes me in, "I love you, Ripper."

I lean in, taking her mouth for moment. "And I've got a big cock?" I ask, making her snort.

"You know you do."

"I love you, too, babe."

"Yeah?"

I nod. "With every beat of my heart. You're my woman, my ol' lady. The diamond I found in the rough, and I'm not ever letting you go."

She rewards me with a beautiful, blistering white smile. "All right, Ripper. I can meet your mom now. I just hope she likes me, because I'm never giving you up either," she remarks with a touch of sexy as fuck sass. She grabs a towel and leaves me in the shower for an impromptu jackoff session. Thanks to the show I get while watching her wiggle her ass and tits into her clothes, I manage to come in about four minutes. Embarrassing stats to a man, but one hell of a compliment to the woman in question.

"Baby!" My mother coos toward me and leaps off her barstool. She's got Powerhouse, Blow, and Whiskey all around her. I bet she was sucking up their attention too. "I figured you sweet boys would be hungry. I stopped by Shipley's since they're the best, brought a couple dozen donuts and kolaches."

Whiskey sips his coffee, then says, "She got the jalapeno sausage kind you like."

My mom flashes him a grin. "I know what my son likes."

I pull her in for a hug, pressing a kiss to the top of her head. "Ma. Thanks for the food. You're here early, yeah?"

She slides back on her vacated stool, sharing, "Pop's on a run. You know I get restless when he's not home."

"I told you, let me know this shit, Ma. I could send one of the guys over to check on you."

She pats my chin, and I step away, walking around the bar to get the largest cup of coffee I can find. I pour another cup full, setting them on the bar.

"I have one, baby, but thank you," Ma practically preens, thinking I was getting the cup of coffee for her. I should've at least asked if she wanted some more. I saw the cup sitting in front of her. Whiskey had her one made that has *Ma* on it with a skull and roses. The brothers tend to be soft on her, like she is on them.

Powerhouse coughs, while Blow laughs loudly. Whiskey just raises a brow, silently asking me if I woke my woman up too. I send him a nod and scowl at the other two dipshits. "It's uh, not for you, Ma."

"Hm?"

I start to repeat myself when Alice makes her way in to join us. She approaches my mother with a warm smile, her shoulders back with her confident stride. This isn't my sweet, naïve woman that I brough back to the club with me. This is the senator's daughter. She's in her zone, and being good with people, I don't know why I expected anything less from her. Was I thinking she'd shuffle in and hide behind me? That's not the type of woman I'd ever claim. My ol' lady is a strong bitch.

My woman meets my gaze. "Jenkins sent a text. Baker's coming home today." As much as it pisses me off that her father had his guy send the text to her, I rub the feeling off. It's a day to celebrate if our brother is getting out of lockup. It means Alice's father came through on his end of the bargain.

The brothers around us cheer, knowing what the news means as well, and I flash a grin. I don't respond past that, as it's club business. We'll figure out the details after my mom leaves, and we have a chance to tell the others. We'll need to decide if the entire club will ride out to meet him, or if it should only be a few of us.

My coffee's momentarily forgotten as I step around the bar to Alice. "Ma," I begin, holding my hand out to my woman. She places her palm in mine, and I gesture to her. "This is my *ol' lady*, Gem." I look to my woman, leaning in for a chaste kiss. After I place my peck on her lips, openly stating our relationship to my mother, I say, "Babe, this is my mom. Everybody calls her Ma."

Gem holds her right hand out, expecting to shake my mom's. We're all surprised when Ma jumps off her stool and practically tackles my ol' lady in a hug. I know Ma is a good woman. She's always been welcoming to my brothers. However, I never knew what to expect when it came to me finally taking on an ol' lady.

Gem wraps her free hand around Ma, flashing me a shocked smile as my mom holds her tightly. They draw back from each other, my woman's eyes wide as Ma comes away with tears cresting. She places a wrinkled palm to Alice's cheek, as we all watch with rapt fascination.

"It's a pleasure to meet you. Ripper told me how you stop by often, and I'm so happy you came today."

Ma's watery hazel gaze meets mine for a beat before landing back on Alice. "*His ol' lady*," she whispers in awe.

"I-I know this must have taken you off guard," Gem stammers, not knowing how to react to the attention.

Ma offers her a tender smile. "Shh, baby. I'm just so happy for my boy. I've been praying for the day he'd meet the right woman." She drops her hand away, pulling my girl in for another hug and says, "Welcome to the family, Gem." Then she's reaching for me next, whispering how proud she is of me and how happy she is for us finding each other. Never in a million years did I think I could ever feel this much love inside my clubhouse. Sure, the brothers have a rough sort of love for each other, but coming from my ol' lady and my mom, together, in one room…it's overwhelming.

Ma releases us, quickly swiping away her tears. She snatches up Gem's hand. "You boys have more donuts, I want to visit with my daughter-in-law." She tugs her over to the table, calling out for us to bring them some coffee. Gem offers me a shocked smile, happiness radiating from her. She's so beautiful in my club, surrounded by my people.

The brothers and I silently gape at each other. We're not used to not being the center of Ma's attention. And she's already calling her a daughter-in-law. I can't help but shake my head. Obviously, Ma's made up her mind that not only will Alice wear my patch, but also my ring. Not that I mind in the slightest, but we'll get to that when we're both ready.

"Looks like she's got a new favorite," Whiskey mutters, and I can't be upset about it in the slightest.

My mother's the best woman I know, aside from my woman. If there's anyone who can show Gem the ropes of being an ol' lady and offer her the shoulder she may need in this life, it's Ma. My ol' lady couldn't be in better hands, and that's a damn good feeling. Alice may have lost the constant contact and unhealthy control from her father, but she's gained the support of my family. Unlike her father, my mom will love and protect her like her own. I was skeptical before, but there isn't a doubt in my mind anymore.

Gem is mine, and I'm hers. I'm a selfish bastard, so I'll never give her up. The Royal Bastards have their first ol' lady, and she's a fucking queen.

The End!

Thank you for reading Bastard! I truly hope you enjoyed this story and want more from this crew. I plan to write another novel, maybe add in some more about Maddy, or maybe wait awhile on her ending. I can't seem to write a standalone to save my life, I always end up wanting more from the other characters. The next in the series is scheduled to release November 2020, so keep your fingers crossed that I can make it happen. As always, thanks for sticking with me until the end. I hope this book motivates you to keep reading more from me. If you're a new reader and love MC, please check out my Oath Keepers MC series as well.

Any reviews help an author—short or long—but please, no spoilers! XO- Sapphire

Also By Sapphire

Oath Keepers MC Series

Secrets

Exposed

Relinquish

Forsaken Control

Friction

Princess

Sweet Surrender – free short story

Love and Obey – free short story

Daydream

Baby

Chevelle

Cherry

Heathen

Russkaya Mafiya Series

Secrets

Corrupted

Corrupted Counterparts – free short story

Unwanted Sacrifices

Undercover Intentions

Dirty Down South Series

Freight Train

3 Times the Heat

2 Times the Bliss

Complete Standalones

Gangster

Unexpected Forfeit

The Main Event – free short story

Oath Keepers MC Collection

Russian Roulette

Tease – Short Story Collection

Oath Keepers MC Hybrid Collection

Vendetti

Viking - free newsletter short story

Capo Dei Capi Vendetti Duet

The Vendetti Empire - part 1

The Vendetti Queen - part 2

The Vendetti Seven (Coming Soon)

Harvard Academy Elite Duet

Little White Lies

Ugly Dark Truth

Royal Bastards MC TEXAS

Bastard

Kings of Carnage MC Series

Bash – Vice President

More Royal Bastards from other Authors

Read more about Gamble in Bet on Me -5 stars from Sapphire!
(Royal Bastards MC: Baltimore)
Hart

My prez thinks I betrayed his trust, but I didn't.

I did the only thing I could think of at the time. I went to the one person who just might believe my ass, the National Charter Prez, Rancid. Fortunately for me, he believed every word I told him and had me lay low for a while.

The plan he made was foolish at best and got me in deeper shit than I was in before. Now that Rancid's gone, our new National Charter Prez, Jameson, is having me patch into another charter. One where I'll be free to be who I am. What a load of shit that is. Or at least, it's what I thought.

I'm a dead man, but none of it matters when my eyes see the one thing I'd gamble with.

Her. Add to your TBR here: https://bit.ly/2O4TpUd

Other Royal Bastard Charters:

Erin Trejo: Blood Lust

Chelle C Craze & Eli Abbott: Bad Like Me

K Webster: Koyn (FIVE STARS FROM SAPPHIRE)

Esther E. Schmidt: Petros

Elizabeth Knox: Bet On Me (FIVE STARS FROM SAPPHIRE)

Glenna Maynard: Lady & the Biker (FIVE STARS FROM SAPPHIRE)

Madison Faye: Filthy Bastard

CM Genovese: Frozen Rain (FOUR STARS FROM SAPPHIRE)

J. Lynn Lombard: Blayze's Inferno

Crimson Syn: Inked In Vengeance

Addison Jane: Her Ransom

Izzy Sweet & Sean Moriarty: Broken Wings

Sapphire Knight

Nikki Landis: Ridin' For Hell

KL Ramsey: Savage Heat

M. Merin: Axel

Sapphire Knight: Bastard

Bink Cummings: Switch Burn

Winter Travers: Playboy

Linny Lawless: The Heavy Crown

Jax Hart: Desert King

Elle Boon: Royally Broken

Kristine Allen: Voodoo

Ker Dukey: Animal

KE Osborn: Defining Darkness

Shannon Youngblood: Silver & Lace

BASH

By Sapphire Knight

Bash

Sweet Savannah Mae hit me out of nowhere...or, I should say, I hit her—literally. My bike smashed right into her. Talk about a way to make a lasting impression. One look at her, and I swore I'd met an angel. She was the light to my dark that stirred up emotions I didn't think I possessed.

In a blink, Savannah becomes everything to me. When I find out the truth she's hiding, it rocks my world. I'm the vice president of the Kings of Carnage MC—a spot I've earned. If any man thinks they can harm what's mine, they've got another thing coming.

But, so do I, because Savannah isn't all she seems. No, my woman's an angel with a spine of steel. She doesn't need a knight in shining armor to save her. She needs a pair of wings to help her fly.

-A Gritty MC romance with a brand-new club, characters, and storyline.

-Bash is a complete standalone that does not need any other books read prior.

-Steamy romantic suspense full of action, alpha bad boys, and strong women.

Gear up for an explosive new series from 6 bestselling Authors you love!

Hilary Storm - President, Sapphire Knight - Vice President, Chelsea Camaron - Road Captain, M.N. Forgy - Enforcer, Nicole James - Treasurer, Kim Jones

Acknowledgements

My husband – This life wouldn't be possible without having your continued support. I know it's not always easy when I zone out on my laptop and don't want to be disturbed. I appreciate you rolling with it and embracing my chosen career. I'm glad you've discovered a way to implement Knight Creations business to fit so well with mine. I wouldn't want to spend my life with anyone else. I love you, and I'm thankful for you. I can't say it enough.

My boys – You're my whole world. I love you both. This never changes, and you better not be reading these books until you're thirty and tell yourself your momma did not write them! I can never express how grateful I am for your support. You are quick to tell me that my career makes you proud, that I make you proud. As far as mom wins go, that one takes the cake. I love you with every beat of my heart, and I will forever.

My Beta Babes –This wouldn't be possible without you always being there to cheer me on. I can't express my gratitude enough for each of you. I'm blessed to have your continued support. Thank you Jay, Kathren, Tara, Lindsey, and Tina for reading Bastard so quickly and offering me your thoughts. I appreciate your help with the blurb, also Hilary Storm, Victoria Ashley and my awesome editor Mitzi.

Editor Mitzi Carroll – Your hard work makes mine stand out, and I'm so grateful! Thank you for pouring tons of hours into my passion and being so wonderful to me. Thank you for your amazing support and always being there whenever I need you.

Marisa Nichols Proofreading/Alated Bibliophile thank you for proofreading Bastard, I enjoy reading your comments with Mitzi's. You two make my day! It's an honor to have you two in my corner.

A big thank you to Crimson Syn for inviting me to be a part of the Royal Bastards World!

To my sweet friend and kick ass Author, Elizabeth Knox, thank you for coming together on this one. I had so much fun putting our characters in each other's books and I hope we do it again in the future. I can't thank you enough for all the support and kindness you've showed me. You are truly a great person and I'm so happy you came into my life.

Laura Shelnutt thank you for always having my back! It's wonderful people like you that make it so I can continue to do what I love. You are awesome and I can't wait to hug you the next time I see you. Until then, keep being freaking awesome.

My Blogger Friends – YOU ARE AMAZING! No, really, you are. You take a new chance on me with each book and in return, share my passion with the world. You never truly get enough credit, and I'm forever grateful! There are so many of you that have stuck with me from the beginning. That dedication is truly humbling.

My Readers – I love you. You make my life possible, thank you. I can't wait to meet many of you this year and in the future. To those of you leaving me the awesome spoiler free reviews, you motivate me to keep writing. For that, I will forever be grateful, as this is my passion in life.

And as always, ADOPT DON'T SHOP! Save a life today and adopt from a rescue or your local animal shelter.
#ProudDobermanMom

Stay up to date with Wall Street Journal and USA Today Bestselling Author Sapphire Knight:

Website

www.authorsapphireknight.com

Newsletter

bit.ly/SKnightNewsletter

Facebook

www.facebook.com/AuthorSapphireKnight

BookBub

www.bookbub.com/profile/sapphire-knight

Instagram:

http://instagram.com/authorsapphireknight

Printed in Great Britain
by Amazon